"Are you challenging me to a showdown?"

Dane asked softly as his finger trailed lightly down Ashley's neck, making her shiver with uncontrollable awareness.

"H-hardly!" she stuttered, hastily retreating from the stand she had just taken. "That would be silly, especially when you've already warned me that I wouldn't like the consequences." A statement she didn't doubt in the slightest!

"All that submissiveness," he drawled lazily, "when in reality we both know that you'd love nothing better than to see me hanged, drawn and quartered!"

"You've got me all wrong," Ashley said, glancing at him demurely from under her lashes. When his eyes narrowed doubtfully, she disclosed, "I'm not that greedy—hanging will do!"

OTHER
Harlequin Romances
by KERRY ALLYNE

Many of these titles are available at your local bookseller
or through the Harlequin Reader Service.

For a free catalogue listing all available Harlequin Romances,
send your name and address to:

HARLEQUIN READER SERVICE,
M.P.O. Box 707, Niagara Falls, N.Y. 14302
Canadian address: Stratford, Ontario, Canada N5A 6W2

or use coupon at back of book.

West of the Waminda

by

KERRY ALLYNE

Harlequin Books

TORONTO • LONDON • NEW YORK • AMSTERDAM
SYDNEY • HAMBURG • PARIS

Original hardcover edition published in 1978
by Mills & Boon Limited

ISBN 0-373-02248-4

Harlequin edition published March 1979

Printed in U.S.A.

CHAPTER ONE

Oh, God, wasn't it ever going to rain again? Ashley Beaumont dragged her hat from her blonde head, wiped the back of her hand across a perspiring forehead, and despondently settled the wide felt covering back into place. For three years the district had been without decent rain now, and still there wasn't a cloud in sight to mar that cobalt canopy overhead or which could give rise to even the smallest spark of optimism. Oh, they'd had storms all right—willy-willies which sprang up out of nowhere to swirl dust, twigs, and bone-dry grass into whirlwinds of hot, choking grittiness; and dry storms that rent the skies apart with ear-splitting crescendoes, accompanied by jagged forks of lightning which were only too filling to set fire to what little feed there was left in the arid paddocks. But no rain.

During these last summers they had been keeping an even closer watch than usual on the cyclone depressions which harried the coasts of Western Australia and the Northern Territory at this time of year. The western plains of New South Wales might have been over a thousand miles away, but those awesome storms were often the only means of restoring the life-giving moisture to the dry inland areas as they blew their way into rain squalls once they moved overland and headed east across the continent.

She sighed and turned with a wan smile to the dark-skinned man beside her. 'Well, I think that's about all we can do for today, Ted,' she murmured tiredly, flexing aching shoulder muscles. 'If we lop those wilgas any further they'll never survive.'

His generously greying head nodded in agreement as the old stockman's eyes roamed over the last tree they had cut back. Stock loved the foliage of the normally rounded little wilga tree, and although it was long regarded as an extremely useful form of fodder in time of drought, discretion still had to be used in its cutting.

'Reckon so, Ashley, although there's still those left in the high paddock. They might keep them going a bit longer,' he replied consolingly as they made their way slowly back to the ute, once white but now covered with patches of rust and turning bronze in the rays of a brilliantly setting sun.

'I suppose so,' she conceded with an attempted cheerfulness she was far from feeling. But for how much longer? And after that—then what? She shook her head and refused to think that far ahead. Maybe by then the rain would have arrived.

Perhaps that was what Ted was thinking too. Ashley flicked a glance from the windscreen to the lined face of the Aboriginal sitting beside her. Dear Ted, whatever would they have done without him? He and his wife, Nellie, had been working on Kindyerra when Ashley's father bought the property some eighteen years before, and were now the only employees left—the rest had had to be put off long ago when things started going bad—but Ted had been around ever since she could remember. It had been Ted who showed her how to ride, Ted who taught her all there was to know about stock work, and Ted who instilled in her his own concern for, and love of, the land.

Her father, although she had been too young to realise it at the time, hadn't been interested enough to learn any of those things for himself, let alone impart them to any of his children. Howard Beaumont had merely wanted to look the part of the wealthy grazier—made possible in those early years by funds received from the estate on the death of his father-in-law—without having the slightest desire to acquire any of the knowledge or skills necessary to make it a permanent way of life. His attitude had always been, 'Leave it to Mother Nature—she's been taking care of these things for years,' with the consequence that the well kept property they had moved on to slowly, but surely, began to deteriorate. In the beginning, of course, it hadn't been quite so noticeable, but his practice of selling stock when he wanted more ready money and then replacing it later—

and usually at three times the price—steadily began to make deep inroads into the station's profits.

Looking back, Ashley had long since come to the conclusion that she hadn't helped matters either. She was the third child in a family of four; her elder brother and two sisters had taken very little interest in anything rural, and it had almost been as if her father was seeking a reflected glory with regard to his second daughter's pastoral accomplishments, with the result that he took her everywhere with him, boasting to his cronies about her newest proficiency and showering her with expensive presents in praise. Not that he was any less benevolent with the rest of his family, because he had certainly never been mean with his money, it was just that he liked to spend big— but, unfortunately, not always wisely—and by the time she was ten Ashley had been well on her way to becoming an impudently precocious child who, in her father's eyes at least, could do no wrong.

Though it was generally accepted as the passenger's job, it was Ashley who alighted from the ute at the gate leading into the house paddock and swung it wide before driving through and then going back to close it. That Ted, well into his sixties now, could put in a day like they had today in the blazing heat was a credit to his uncomplaining endurance. The least she could do was to save him some energy on the way home.

On this thought, her eyes roved upwards to the white-painted homestead set before them as she slid behind the wheel again and they moved off along the sandy track, her mind once more returning to the past.

That carefree life had departed, suddenly and grimly, upon Howard Beaumont's death from a heart attack when Ashley was fifteen. Only then did the rest of his family come to know the full extent of his extravagances and just how heavily he had mortgaged the property in order to support them in such a gracious style. Ruth Beaumont, Ashley's mother, had had her doubts from time to time that they weren't as prosperous as her husband liked everyone to believe, but even she had been shocked when they dis-

covered the total amount of debts her husband had managed to accrue over the years.

Ashley stopped the vehicle outside Ted's small cottage
and, after exchanging a few pleasantries with Nellie through
the open window, continued on and parked alongside the
family station wagon which was of an even older vintage
than the ute, but luckily suffered very few defects thanks to
her brother Bruce's constant attention.

Experienced eyes ran over the building automatically,
noting where another sheet of iron on the roof had rusted
through and mentally making a note to remind Bruce to fix
it when he was mobile again. Never an enthusiastic rider,
he had been out last weekend checking the water pumps
and bore drains when a snake had startled his mount into
rearing and thereby throwing him on to an old tree stump
which had broken his leg. It was an accident they could well
have done without, thought Ashley morosely as she dragged
weary feet up the steps and across the wide verandah which
completely encircled the house. Bruce might not be the best
stockman in the world, but he was another pair of hands
and he was reliable.

Ruth Beaumont, her blonde hair whitening now, but her
figure still slim and upright, lifted her gaze from where she
had been preparing the evening meal to watch her
daughter's entrance into the kitchen, a worried frown creasing her forehead.

'You're trying to do too much, Ashley,' she cautioned
gently, not for the first time. 'This place is far too big for
you and Ted to attempt to run on your own. It's too much
even when Bruce is able to help, and—and . . .' she hesitated and her eyes took in Ashley's tired appearance sadly,
'I hate to say it, love, but I think it's a losing battle anyway.'

Ashley helped herself to a cup of tea from the pot on the
old-fashioned dresser and hunched her shoulders dejectedly
before dropping on to a chair by the table.

'Maybe, Mum, maybe. But it's got to rain *some* time,' she
forecast wryly.

'But not necessarily this year—or next—or even within the next seven, for that matter,' her mother returned with a knowledge born of previous experience, and resumed chopping the vegetables she had laid out on the table. 'And even if it rained tomorrow we still wouldn't have anywhere near the amount required for our next mortgage repayment.'

'I know,' Ashley conceded heavily, her soft lips pulling in worriedly at the corners. 'It's just that I can't bear the thought of leaving here. It's the only home I can ever remember and I love it.' She gave a poor copy of her once impudent grin. 'And I guess it's partly because I hate to have to admit that I'm defeated—that this damned unpredictable weather of ours has finally beaten me!'

'Sometimes it's better to cut your losses than throw good money after bad,' came softly, tentatively.

'You think we ought to sell?' Ashley enquired expressionlessly.

Ruth raised her head again to survey the wary features turned towards her; the wide spaced blue eyes with their long dark lashes and delicately arching brows, the slightly retroussé nose above the shapely mouth and small pointed chin.

'I certainly think we should give it serious consideration,' she nodded eventually.

It wasn't that she wanted to give up their home any more than her daughter did, but she couldn't see the sense in continuing when, to her mind, the final outcome was inevitable. What was needed to put this property back on its feet again was a large injection of money, which they surely didn't have, and the manpower to keep it a paying proposition, which wasn't within their means either!

Ashley pushed out of her chair and went to stand by the window, looking out over the denuded earth unseeingly, hands thrust into the pockets of her work-stained jeans. 'Have you spoken to the others about it yet?' she asked over one shoulder.

'Not yet,' Ruth shook her head negatively. 'I know what

their answers will be, but I also know the place means more to you, and it was your reaction I was anxious about,' she confessed ruefully.

Pacing past her thoughtfully, Ashley stopped beside her chair and picked up her cup. 'I suppose I have been pretty selfish all these years in making such a fuss about keeping the place, haven't I?' she suggested with genuine contrition.

'No, of course you haven't!' her mother was quick to disagree. 'It would have been to all our benefits if things had turned out differently, and goodness knows you've worked harder than any of us to make a go of it!'

'Who's working harder than any of us? Ash?' a deep voice enquired from the doorway as Bruce Beaumont edged into the room from the hall with the aid of crutches, his left leg encased in a heavy white cast. 'Doesn't she always?' he continued with a grin as he propped himself against the cupboard and poured himself a cup of tea.

At the sight of her brother's thin, sensitive face, Ashley sighed and pulled a self-mocking grimace. 'But only for lost causes, it seems.'

'Had a lousy day, have you, little one?' he sympathised as he stretched out an arm and, catching hold of her shoulder, pulled her comfortingly close to his side. 'I'm sorry I've had to leave you and Ted to it after this,' tapping regretfully at the plaster, 'but I'll soon be back in action and then maybe I can share some of the load with you again.'

'I don't think that's exactly what Ashley was meaning,' Ruth broke in before her daughter could reply. 'I've—I've just been saying that I think it's—it's about time we seriously considered selling Kindyerra,' she told him somewhat hesitantly.

'So-o!' Bruce looked down into his sister's troubled face with commiseration evident in his hazel eyes. 'And what was your answer to *that*, little one?'

Ashley took a mouthful of tea from the cup she was still holding and kept her eyes lowered to the pale tan liquid left. 'I said something to the effect that I—that I . . .' the words stuck in her throat and she had to swallow hard before prevaricating, 'thought it wasn't . . . unreasonable.' But she was immediately glad she had done so when she felt the tenseness leaving Bruce's body.

'You really mean that, Ash?' He tipped her head upwards with a finger under her chin, his gaze intent.

'Yes, I really mean it,' she averred huskily, but was glad when he hugged her close to his chest so that he couldn't see the brilliance of unshed tears which rushed involuntarily to her eyes. The rest of the family, with perhaps the exception of her mother, would be only too pleased to see the property sold, so how could she have said otherwise when the future looked so grim?

Bruce was still holding her tightly when their younger sister, Janelle, banged in through the verandah screen door with a bucket in her hand. One puzzled glance took in Bruce and Ashley, then carried on to her mother.

'Okay, I give up,' she spoke out cheerfully. 'What's been going on while I've been trying to coax some milk out of that almost dry cow?'

'We've just decided it might be time to put Kindyerra up for sale,' Bruce was the one to inform her from above Ashley's head.

'Whacko!' Janelle's obvious agreement with the scheme resounded jubilantly through the room until a warning shake of her mother's head brought other thoughts to mind and she moved across to her sister quickly. 'Gee, I'm sorry, Ashley,' she apologised in a low tone. 'I shouldn't have said that, I know how much you wanted to get the place on to a profit-making basis again.' Then, enquiringly to her mother, 'Isn't there any other way?'

'I'm afraid not, Jan,' Ruth sighed regretfully. 'This drought has destroyed just about any chance we had of getting that mortgage paid off. We're further in debt now than we've ever been.'

A forlorn kind of reprieve occurred to Ashley and after wiping her fingertips surreptitiously across her eyes she eased away from Bruce to ask quietly, 'Do you think we're likely to find a buyer while the station looks as barren as it does?'

'Well, I can't say for certain,' her mother replied cautiously, 'but when Jack Prescott was organising that last loan for us, he did say that he knew of someone who was willing to buy the place if we wanted to sell. I don't know whether the man would still be interested, of course, but I suppose we have nothing to lose if I give Jack a call tomorrow and ask him to make a few enquiries in that direction.'

'And did he also say what price this man would be willing to pay if we did decide to sell? Or will he be hoping to buy us out cheaply just because there happens to be a drought?' Ashley demanded.

Ruth's eyes flickered worriedly to her son and back to Ashley again. 'How can I say until Jack's been in touch with him?' she countered logically. 'For all we know he may not even be interested any more.'

'I guess so, and . . . I'm sorry, Mum,' Ashley immediately felt remorse for her bitter questions and gave her parent a wry smile. 'Perhaps I'd better go and have a shower so I can cool off, otherwise I might be tempted to come up with any number of reasons why we shouldn't go ahead with the idea after all,' as she spun on her heel and hurried out of the room without giving anyone a chance to reply.

In the bathroom she stripped off her grubby working clothes and stepped beneath the cascading water, appreciative at least that the house bore was still managing to supply its usual volume of water even if it wasn't as cold as she would have liked. After soaping the dust and perspiration away from her skin she rubbed shampoo vigorously into her hair in an effort to rid it of every last particle of the fine powder which seemed to hover above the landscape these days whether a wind was blowing or not. Normally she preferred her waving hair long, but since the drought that hadn't been practical and now she kept it much shorter so that it curled about her scalp like a sleek silky cap.

Back in her bedroom she took a faded and well-washed blue and white check shift from her wardrobe and slipped it over her lissome form, combed her towelled hair into shape and applied a pale pink lipstick, her eyes seeing things they hadn't really had time to notice for many months now— the wallpaper which badly needed renewing, the worn carpet, the paintwork which had bubbled and flaked in numerous places, and the tears in the flyscreen which enclosed the verandah and were easily visible through the open doors beside her dressing table. She let out a deep breath heavily. Not since a couple of years before her father died had there really been any repairs or renovations made to the homestead, and it was starting to show— glaringly.

Even though the three of them had taken jobs in town— Janelle had wanted to as well, but it wasn't until a month or so ago that she had completed her last year in high school, and their elder sister, Lori, was married and had her own household to care for—the repayments on the loan took most of whatever they earned, and what was left had been needed to pay Ted and Nellie or had been put back into the property. There were always dipping and drenching chemicals to buy, or replacement parts for ageing machinery, shearing fees, and taxes. Luckily, Bruce was mechanically minded, otherwise they would have had to pay out for repairs to pumps, motors, and the vehicles too.

In the circumstances, perhaps it wasn't so surprising that the homestead had fared so badly, but then it was no worse off than they themselves, Ashley mused, fingering the thin material of the dress she was wearing. They hadn't been lavish in that direction either, only buying new clothes when it was absolutely necessary and making do for the rest of the time. She really couldn't remember the last time she had bought a new dress for wearing out—it had only been working gear she had purchased during these last dispiriting years. Not that she had begrudged any of the inconveniences or compromises, because it had been a labour of love with owning Kindyerra free and clear the ultimate goal, but the drought had pushed that possibility further and further into the distance with each week it persisted, until now ... How could she bear the thought of leaving altogether?

'Does this mean I'll be able to take that hairdressing apprenticeship that Jean Shawcross offered me, after all?' Janelle asked excitedly once the evening meal was concluded and they were stacking the used plates in the sink. Previously it had been decided that she wouldn't receive enough money from an apprenticeship and that it would be preferable if she sought another position which paid a little better.

'I—well, I hadn't got around to thinking about that yet,' her mother responded a little flusteredly. 'I—I suppose you could—provided we do get a buyer, of course,' she added a dampening warning.

'But if I don't let her know for certain within the next few weeks she'll employ someone else,' lamented Janelle with a crestfallen look at seeing her prized occupation being snatched away from under her nose.

Ruth clucked sympathetically but couldn't be swayed. 'I'm sorry, Jan, but we can't just stop working the property because it's going up for sale. You know as well as we do that it's not a seller's market at the moment, and if we can't find a buyer then we're going to have to keep on working it ourselves.'

Janelle opened her mouth to plead her cause once again and then closed it, knowing her mother had spoken nothing but the truth, but on seeing her sister's deep disappointment Ashley decided it was time she spoke up on her behalf.

'Oh, go on, Mum, let her take it,' she urged with an encouraging smile. 'We all know Jan has never wanted to be anything else ever since she first started school, and we'll find someone who wants the place sooner or later. Everyone knows this land west of the Waminda river is some of the best in the State, and even though it might not look much at the moment, that's not going to stop someone who knows what he's about and has an eye for the future,' she concluded with plausible reasoning.

'But, Ashley, what about you and Ted?' her mother protested. 'You badly need extra help out there, and especially now that Bruce has broken his leg.'

'Oh, I expect we'll manage somehow. We had to while

Jan was finishing school, and this time it won't be indefinitely, will it?' Ashley defended her stand pensively, but was rewarded by the gratitude apparent in her sister's glowing brown eyes, and went on, 'Which reminds me ... has anyone mentioned anything about this to Ted and Nellie yet?'

Ruth moved her head slowly from side to side. 'No, I thought it might be best coming from you. You've been closer to him than any of us and I think he would prefer it if you were the one to break the news.'

'Probably,' Ashley nodded in agreement. 'I'll go down and see him once we've finished this,' as she picked up a tea towel and began wiping the first of the dishes her mother stood in the draining tray.

The night air was cool against her skin when Ashley picked her way by moonlight past the outbuildings and down the uneven track to where the Arnolds' cottage stood between another two unoccupied ones. The lights inside threw a welcoming beam on to the small porch and seeing Ted seated on the top step, contentedly puffing on a much loved, much scarred pipe, she lowered herself down beside him companionably as she had often done in the past.

'Something new come to bother you, eh?' he broke the silence softly and brought an unwilling smile to Ashley's lips. She should have known better than to think she could hide her inner feelings from this wise old man with his so very understanding eyes. How many times before had he accurately suspected when she was troubled?

'You always know, don't you, Ted?' she replied with a question of her own, her fingers tugging at some weedy grass which had somehow managed to survive and was now pushing up between the steps. 'I've often wondered how.'

Ted puffed again on his pipe, his eyelids closing slowly so that Ashley wondered if he was dozing, but then he smiled and gave her an unbelievably alert sideways glance.

'Reading people isn't so different from reading tracks, little missie,' he used the pet name he had been wont to call her by in the days when he had begun her willing education into the ways of nature. 'It's not always a case of looking for the obvious, or for things that are where they shouldn't be. Sometimes it's possible to tell more by looking for those signs which you know should be there—but aren't!'

'And you think something's missing from me tonight that should be there?' she quizzed speculatively.

'There's something missing all right,' he assured her, quietly confident in his own perception. 'We just put in one of the hardest weekends we've ever had, yet when you left me this afternoon, you might have been bone tired, but you still had that look about you that you weren't beaten. That look's gone now!'

Ashley's mouth tightened at the corners. 'We've—um—decided to put Kindyerra up for sale, Ted,' she relayed dully.

'A-h-h!' There was an enormous depth of feeling, and understanding, in that drawn-out exclamation. 'I thought it wouldn't be long in coming. But you can't blame them, they . . .'

'I *don't* blame them, Ted,' she interrupted hastily. 'It's just that . . .'

'It wasn't your way out of the problem and you love the place too much to want to leave it,' he finished for her.

She spread her hands wide helplessly. 'But what else can I do?' she cried.

'Nothing, little missie, you've done all you can,' his hard calloused hand touched her gently on the arm. 'It's not right that you should waste all your youth by trying to do a man's work. I'm afraid this land needs stronger backs than yours, or mine, to put it right again from here. You go with them,' a movement of his head indicated the homestead, 'and start being a carefree young girl again. It's a long time since you've had anything to laugh about, and that's not as it should be. Kindyerra will survive—you'll see.'

'I don't think I could stand the thought of someone else owning it,' she confessed broodingly.

One dark hand was held repressively high. 'Now you're

letting the land own you, Ashley, and that's not good. You should be satisfied just knowing that it will be well cared for in future.'

'But how can I be sure of that? The next owner might be someone like—like my father. He didn't care for the land.'

The old pipe came into play again and his eyes half closed as he gazed into the starlit midnight blue sky. 'After the bad comes the good—as it's always done,' he advised with all the forbearance of his ancient race. 'He will care!'

'Now you're going all mystical on me,' she half smiled, then quickly became serious as she enquired anxiously, 'But what will you do, Ted? Will you offer your services to the new owner?'

Stooped shoulders rose philosophically. 'Maybe he will have no need for an old stockman whose working days are numbered and cannot move as well as he used to.'

'Then he'll be a fool!' Ashley flared indignantly. 'You know this property and all its peculiarities better than anyone, and he'll be a poor judge of ability if he doesn't realise that fact!'

'So protective on an old man's behalf. Perhaps today hasn't tired you as much as I believed,' he smiled slyly.

Ashley chuckled vivaciously, something she hadn't done for months. 'And I think you're an old fraud! Although I'm not sure whether you're attempting to play on my sympathy, or to take my mind off other matters,' she grinned, her even white teeth gleaming in the darkness.

'That you, Ashley?' Nellie waddled out on to the porch at the unexpected sound of laughter. Short and fat, but perpetually optimistic, she had never been known to be anything but amiable. 'You think the rain's coming that makes you laugh like that?' she probed.

'No, Nellie, nothing so exciting, I'm sorry to say.' Ashley twisted round to smile up at the woman standing behind her. 'I was telling your husband that he's a fraud.'

'And haven't I been telling you that for years?' Nellie's dark eyes glowed merrily as she turned them on her spouse. 'What's she caught you out at this time, Ted?'

'Only in trying to keep her thoughts away from the fact that they're going to put Kindyerra on the market,' he answered her in a muted undertone.

Nellie's first reaction to the news was much the same as her husband's had been—a long breathless, 'Ah!' followed by, 'That's a shame after the way you've tried to keep it going all these years, and all the effort you've put in. Still, maybe that's the way things were meant to be, what with . . .'

'Nellie!'

There was a sharp note of command in Ted's voice as he cut his wife off in mid-sentence which Ashley had never heard him use before—not to Nellie, anyway—and she dropped her gaze to his in puzzlement.

In return he merely shrugged somewhat embarrassedly and waved his hands in an apologetic motion. 'I just thought there'd been enough talk about it for one evening,' he excused himself awkwardly, although Nellie promptly supported his explanation with a vindicating, 'Of course—I should have known better—you'd only just finished telling me that you'd been trying to occupy her mind with something else.'

A little less perplexed but still a trifle surprised, Ashley looked from one to the other and uttered a small deprecatory laugh. 'I know I might not like talking about it, but you really don't have to wrap me in cotton wool. I shall have to come to terms with it sooner or later.'

'But not tonight,' Ted stated firmly. 'There'll be plenty of time for that before a sale goes through.'

'I guess so.' Ashley rose to her feet and rubbed the palms of her hands down the side of her dress, strangely ill at ease all of a sudden. 'Anyway, I suppose I'd better be getting back to the house. It's work in town again tomorrow and if I don't want to sleep in I'd better not leave it too long before getting to bed. So I'll say goodnight and see you later,' she laughed nervously and raised her right hand in farewell.

Their fond replies and adjurations to 'Sleep well,' floated up the path behind her, but Ashley only half heard them, so engrossed was she with her own confused thoughts.

The rest of the family were watching a movie on T.V. in the lounge when she reached the house and Bruce pulled her down on to the arm of his easy chair as she passed him, his face turning up to hers interestedly.

'How did Ted and Nellie take the news ... okay?' he asked.

'I think so,' she lifted one shoulder indecisively. 'Ted went all profound on me. You know how he sometimes does? And Nellie—well, she started to say something obscure about maybe that's the way it was meant to be, when suddenly he chopped her off and said he didn't think we should talk any more about it tonight. I wasn't sure what to make of it in the end,' she shrugged again, and sighed gloomily.

'Well, I shouldn't let it worry you too much. You know they both like to appear incomprehensible at times,' he smiled soothingly.

'But never on matters as important as this, Bruce! I felt as if ... oh, I don't know what I felt. But *something* just wasn't right!' she tried to explain as rationally as she could.

'I told you that you were working too hard,' Ruth now entered the conversation on a worried note. 'I think it's probably all in your imagination due to your being over-wrought at the idea of us selling.'

'Overwrought!' Ashley echoed, her eyes opening wide in astonishment. 'Oh, Mum, what a description,' she couldn't help laughing. 'But I can assure you that wasn't the case in this instance because, I'll have you know, I don't get over-wrought, as you put it.'

'But you do feel very deeply about this property, Ashley.' Her mother apparently still wasn't fully convinced.

'Well, of course I do—and nor have I ever tried to hide it. But that doesn't mean I'm going to start imagining things directly we talk about moving. You're making me sound like some melodramatic halfwit who's about to fall into an eighteenth-century decline!' she protested re-proachfully.

Janelle's uncontrollable gurgle at this remark had her

mother's face relaxing into a smile too. 'All right, I apologise for implying you might not have heard correctly. No doubt we'll discover what the truth of the matter is all in due course,' Ruth finally conceded. 'Perhaps it was just their way of protecting your feelings in view of the disappointment they must know you're experiencing.'

'That's something similar to what Ted insinuated,' revealed Ashley reflectively.

'There you are, then, that settles that,' her brother grinned as he removed his hand from her waist and prepared to heave himself out of the chair. 'Now, I don't know about the rest of you, but I'm for bed.'

'Might as well, the film's finished,' agreed Janelle as she switched off the T.V. before giving Ashley a hand to help lever Bruce to his feet. 'I'd like to get into town as early as possible tomorrow, then Jean might let me start straight away in the salon. At least that would save me having to check if someone was coming out this way who could give me a lift home, or else filling in time in the library until you're all ready to leave.'

'Quite the eager beaver, isn't she?' Bruce laughed down at Ashley. 'I wonder how long she'll keep it up.'

'You're a great one to talk,' Janelle immediately retorted with a knowing grin. 'You're never happier than when you're toiling away in that hot, greasy garage in town. I don't seem to remember you looked quite so joyful when Ash asked you to give her a hand with the mulesing and tailing of last year's lambs!'

'Ah, well, I guess we all work best at what we enjoy most,' he accepted her laughing retaliation in good part. 'It's only Mum and poor old Ashley who would rather not be employed in Willow Bend,' with his hand compassionately rumpling Ashley's blonde hair as her expression turned to one of obvious distaste.

It wasn't that Tony Mancinelli's restaurant was an unpleasant place to work, just the opposite, in fact, because he was a very thoughtful and friendly employer, but how could she take any enjoyment from waiting on others when her thoughts refused to stay confined within the four walls of that expensive little eating house, and remained defiantly on wide open spaces with constant reminders of what needed to be done on the property?

If they hadn't needed the money so badly she would probably never have given waitressing a second thought, but she had never wanted a formal training in any profession other than one connected with stock work and so, when circumstances beyond the family's control had dictated that she seek additional employment, there hadn't been much choice available. It had been much the same in her mother's case too. Long known as one of the finest cooks in the district, when she had decided to help supplement their income this had been the obvious avenue she pursued, with the result that she also had become one of Tony's employees.

CHAPTER TWO

THE following days passed agonisingly slowly for Ashley. Monday had brought her mother's news—unpleasant for her, but encouraging for the others—that Jack Prescott believed his one-time prospective purchaser for the property might still be interested and that he would see about contacting him as soon as possible.

Tuesday had been one of those days when she would gladly have quit her job if such an action had been thinkable. From the time the restaurant opened in the morning until Bruce collected her mother and herself in the late afternoon, there seemed to have been nothing but complaints from the customers. Either the curry was too hot, or it wasn't hot enough; the steaks were too rare, or they were overdone; they hadn't wanted cooked vegetables with their meal, they'd wanted salad; little Penelope hadn't ordered apple pie and cream, she'd ordered a banana sundae—and that after the atrocious child had kept her standing by the table for a full three minutes while she deliberated between the two! With all the running back and forth she had been forced to do, Ashley had felt it wasn't surprising her feet had ached all the way home with an intensity she hadn't before experienced, not even after the most gruelling hours put in on Kindyerra.

Now it was Wednesday and she pressed her foot down on the accelerator, anxious as always to swiftly cover the fifty miles which would take them to their gateway, and then it was only another six to the homestead. Half her working week had gone and a small pleased smile lit her features at the thought. It was also the day that her elder sister, Lori, and her family came out for dinner, which meant that there would be no rushing around as soon as they arrived in order to prepare the evening meal because Lori would already have seen to it. Which, in turn, gave Ashley more time to speak with Ted and catch up on what he had accomplished during the day and to ascertain what needed to be attended to the following day.

Not quite an hour later she drew to a halt so that Janelle could open the gate leading on to the property, and automatically checked the large wooden-constructed mailbox which stood by the roadway, even though she knew that Lori would have picked up anything which had been left there when she came through before them. Another three stops for gates followed and then they were driving through the house paddock and Lori's two children, Emma and Niall, were rushing out of the house to greet them.

The kitchen was alive with voices when Ashley entered it after parking the wagon within the shaded interior of the shed and walking back to the homestead unhurriedly in deference to the heat which had been inflammably high since early that morning. But she had hardly shut the screen door behind her than Lori—at twenty-nine, seven years Ashley's senior, but with the same deep blue eyes and blonde hair, only hers was a shade darker—had thrust a glass of something refreshingly cold into her hand, given her an affectionate hug in greeting, and exclaimed, 'Mum's just told me that she's planning to sell this place at last! That decision came about rather suddenly, didn't it?'

'Sort of,' Ashley agreed ruefully. Over the last three days she had found herself becoming used to this question as more and more people came to hear of the intention. 'But things weren't getting any better, and so . . .' she allowed her explanation to trail off significantly, knowing her sister would be able to fill in the missing details for herself.

Lori nodded her comprehension and then grinned teasingly. 'Never mind, love, at least I know of one person who'll be only too pleased to have you move into town.' But at the frowning look of blankness she received in response, 'Good heavens, Ash! Although I've often wondered what you see in him, you *do* spend every Thursday evening with Ralph Skinner, don't you?'

With a laugh for her own obtuseness, Ashley inclined her head half sardonically. 'I do, but the fact had slipped my mind for the moment. Why? Were you beginning to think I was making it all up?'

'No, of course not! Seeing that you sleep at our place on Thursdays that might be a little hard to do,' Lori retorted. 'But it did make me wonder if things were cooling off between the pair of you.' Her eyes held Ashley's searchingly as she probed gently, 'Are they?'

Saved the necessity of replying to a question she wasn't sure she knew the answer to by her brother-in-law, Alec Underwood, claiming his wife's attention, Ashley sipped abstractedly at her drink and thought about the matter. It was true that for the last few months she hadn't looked forward to Ralph's company with such spontaneity as she had earlier in their acquaintanceship, but she had been putting that down to a combination of worry over the property and the amount of work to be done making her more tired than usual. Now she wasn't so certain. Perhaps there was some other, entirely different reason after all. She shook her head to break her train of thought and rinsed her empty glass before placing it in the sink. There would be plenty of time to dissect her feelings later, when they didn't have guests.

Intent on changing out of the royal blue and white uniform she was required to wear to work, Ashley exchanged belated kisses with Alec on her way through the kitchen, but was delayed when she reached the hall by Emma and Niall asking if they could ride Amarina down to the lagoon —now empty—and give her a roll in the sand. One of the last presents her father had given her, the black mare was still one of the best stock horses they had left and liked nothing better than a vigorous roll after a hot day.

'Okay,' she consented to their request with a smile. 'As long as you give her a good rub down when you come back and don't let her drink too much.'

'We will,' and 'We won't,' came the separate replies to each piece of advice as eight-year-old Emma led her younger brother out on to the verandah, leaving Ashley smiling behind them and knowing that they wouldn't be wasting any of their precious time in saddling the mare but would ride her bareback—the manner in which Ted had originally taught them to ride, as Ashley herself had been, and like a great many other children were taught in the outback.

Presently, once she had showered and changed into a becoming sun-dress printed in a bold flower design and which left creamy brown shoulders bare, Ashley met Janelle on her way out of the kitchen and obviously preparing to follow her sister's lead. But when their paths would have crossed Janelle caught hold of Ashley's arm and nodded her head back in the direction from which she had just come.

'Lori says she has something *very* interesting to tell us tonight,' she grinned in remembrance of her eldest sister's air of mystery. 'Says it's too sensational to be passed around in bits and pieces and she's going to wait until we're all together before she lets us in on the secret. I think she's after the biggest audience she can get in order to make it more impressive,' her brown eyes twinkled.

'Maybe she's pregnant again,' suggested Ashley dryly, but after her first choked chuckle of laughter Janelle shook her head emphatically.

'No, it's not that, because you know what Lori's like when she finds out she's expecting—it's quite impossible for her to wait to tell everyone. No, it's something else this time, but,' she hunched her shoulders lightly, 'she absolutely refused to give me a clue as to what it might be.'

'Oh, well, that's Lori all over. She always has known what's happening in the district long before anyone else. If it wasn't for the fact that she happens to be my dearly beloved sister, I would be tempted to call her the biggest gossip in Willow Bend,' Ashley teased, but with a broad smile taking any criticism out of her words.

Janelle concurred with a knowledgeable, 'Mmm, that's true,' then carried on irrepressibly, 'but I must be just as bad, because I'm dying to hear what she has to say,' before releasing Ashley's arm with a laugh and hurrying on up the hall towards her room.

Ashley shook her head in mock despair and headed for Ted's cottage. *She* was more interested in learning how the water and feed were holding out in the Stony Gully pad-dock. If they were too low—as she half expected—they would have another active weekend ahead of them in mustering and moving the sheep out before they lost any more of their already depleted flock.

The talk during the meal centred mainly around what the family would do when Kindyerra was finally sold, and though it certainly wasn't a subject which appealed to Ashley she deliberately forced herself to appear interested, aware as she was of her mother's eyes constantly focusing in her direction, the concern therein easily detectable.

'Well, what we'll get for the place really depends on whether it's bought on a walk-in/walk-out basis,' Bruce was replying to a question from Alec. 'If it's not, then of course we'll have to sell the stock separately and, with conditions as they are at present, that wouldn't be to our advantage.'

'You can say that again!' Alec assured him pungently. 'Why, do you know I was talking to one of the auctioneers from the saleyards last week and he was telling me that . . .'

Ashley couldn't bear to listen any further and dis-gruntledly tuned herself out of their conversation. If Bruce had been any sort of grazier at all he wouldn't have needed Alec—who was a dentist!—to tell him how bad the market was. He would have known already . . . just as she did!

But it was no good taking out her frustrations on her brother, she decided a few moments later in an effort to calm her heightening emotions. And it wasn't fair to blame him for not taking more of an interest in the place either. He was entitled to choose what he wanted to do with his life just the same as she was.

Thankfully, while the table was cleared, the coffee poured, and the children departed to watch T.V., Janelle changed the subject to one which revolved around the intricacies of hairdressing techniques, but in the lull which ensued as milk and sugar were passed across the table, Lori's voice sounded dramatically intriguing.

'Guess who I bumped into in town this afternoon?' she charged animatedly.

About to drink from her cup, Ashley looked up to find Lori's eyes concentrating directly on her and after flashing a glance at the others seated round the table her arched brows rose expressively and she enquired banteringly, 'Was that question meant specifically for me ... or can anyone answer?'

'No, it's open for anyone who can come up with the right name,' Lori returned airily, clearly enjoying the puzzled effect she was creating, and concluded with a subtle, 'I just thought you might be interested more than most, that's all.'

'I can't think why. There's no one ...' Ashley began, only to be interrupted by Janelle's curious, 'Male or female?'

For a time it seemed as if Lori couldn't decide whether to give them such a clue or not, but eventually she allowed, 'Male,' in a guarded tone, and was instantly deluged with a variety of names from everyone present, all of which she laughingly discounted.

'You're never going to guess!' she declared triumphantly some minutes later when they had just about exhausted the names they could recall to mind, whereupon Ruth raised one hand in a gesture of defeat and wryly recommended, 'Then I suggest you tell us, Lori, or else we're likely to be playing guessing games all evening.'

Wrinkling her nose in disappointment at having her fun cut short, Lori nevertheless did as her mother had suggested and announced, 'It was ...' but just had to pause before adding a suitably imposing '... *Dane Carmichael!*'

While three voices repeated, 'Dane!' in pleasantly surprised tones, Ashley's fierily resentful, 'Dane Carmichael! What did he have to come back for?' overrode all of them, and a blank-faced Janelle cast bewildered eyes about the room to plaintively request, 'Would someone mind telling me just who is Dane Carmichael?'

'Why don't you ask your sister?' Lori invited, her eyes holding Ashley's provokingly. 'I'm sure she would be only too willing to tell you—if she remembers, that is,' and she chuckled delightedly.

'Remember!' Ashley expostulated indignantly. 'I'll never forget that—that ...' Words failed her momentarily and then she turned to her younger sister to denounce, 'He's a brute and a bully who goes round beating up twelve-year-old girls, and Willow Bend was well rid of him!'

'Oh, come on now, Ash, tell the truth!' Bruce remonstrated with a laugh. 'Dane was never a brute or a bully, and he certainly didn't beat you up.'

'Well, it felt like it at the time,' she retorted in aggrieved accents. 'Don't forget, he was ten years older than I was!'

'And he hit you?' gasped Janelle, shocked.

'Yes, he did! He ...'

'Turned her over his knee and gave her the hiding of her life,' advised Lori, and making Ashley flush angrily at the memory. 'After which he calmly threw her in the dam and drove off without her.'

'Leaving me to *walk* all the way home,' Ashley recalled in disgust.

'From the dam? But ... why?' It was obvious Janelle was finding it all too much to take in.

'Because, I'm sorry to say, your sister asked for it,' her mother put in gently, precipitating a deeply reproachful, 'I did not!' from Ashley, but which Ruth promptly invalidated with a smiling, 'Yes, you did, dear. Not that I think it was altogether your fault, because your father had spoilt you dreadfully by then.'

'In other words, she was an unbearably saucy little baggage!' interpreted Bruce with a grin. 'Only that day she discovered that not everyone was going to accept her impudence without retaliating.'

Ashley presented her brother with a wry grimace. 'Thanks! Remind me to say something nice about you too one of these days!'

Janelle looked at her through new eyes, finding it difficult to imagine Ashley acting in such a manner, and rather disappointed to think that she couldn't remember any of this happening. Now she was avid with curiosity and rushed into asking, 'Why? What did you do?'

A rueful smile caught at Ashley's shapely mouth when she felt herself to be the centre of everyone's attention, and a pink stain of discomposure glowed softly across her cheeks as she shrugged lightly and recounted with determined nonchalance, 'It was one of those scorchingly hot days, so when Dane had loaded the ute with all the rolls of wire, etcetera, he needed to re-fence one of the boundaries in the South Cattle paddock, I went down with him so I could have a swim in the dam.'

'So far, so good,' interposed Lori, and earned herself a speaking glance before Ashley continued.

'Anyway, I was sitting beneath one of the coolibahs, reading a book, by the time he'd made his way back up that end a while later ...'

'Four hours later, to be exact, and it was a hundred and twenty degrees in the shade that day,' Bruce reminded her sardonically, inducing Ashley to abandon what she was saying in order to counter excusingly, 'Well, I didn't know it was that hot!' To which Lori added a teasing, 'Why would you? You'd either been swimming, or sitting in the shade all the time. But do go on, you've just reached the interesting part.'

'I might if you and Bruce would stop interrupting,' was the ironic retort.

'In that case ...' Bruce grinned and swept one hand invitingly wide. 'You have the floor all to yourself, little one. Go to it!'

Ashley's head dipped in response and she turned back to Janelle. 'As I was saying ... I was reading—*Black Beauty*, if I remember correctly—by the time Dane returned, but as he was having some trouble at the corner post he called out for me to get him something from the ute—a pair of fencing pliers, or another wire strainer, I think. Then, when I—I didn't take them over to him, he—he lost his temper and—and hit me,' she finished a trifle evasively.

Her family's reaction was instantaneous, but came in three different forms. Her mother with a softly chiding, 'Ashley love, that's not quite how it was,' while Bruce burst into laughter and exclaimed, 'You conveniently omitted the most relevant part,' and Lori accused, 'Ashley Beaumont! You little fake!' in a shocked voice.

'Then what did happen?' Janelle finally found a space in which to insert her enquiry.

With a remorseful shake of her head, Ashley remained adamantly silent. She didn't relish the memory of the brazen child she had once been, yet contrarily had never allowed herself to forgive, or forget, Dane Carmichael's behaviour either, and so it was left to Bruce to recall the audacious words she had used that hateful day.

'Dane didn't lose his temper because Ashley—who, I might add, thought herself quite the lady of the manor in those days—didn't take him the strainer, but because of the —shall we say, reckless?—remark which accompanied her lack of movement.'

'Which was?' prompted Janelle.

Bruce swung his gaze to Ashley, as if seeking her approval, but she merely hunched her shoulders and gave him an oblique look, and he concluded, 'Which was ... "Get it yourself, that's what you're paid for".'

As she heard this Janelle's eyes opened wide in disbelief and she half choked, half laughed, 'Oh, Ashley, you didn't?'

'Yes, I did! And I'd do it again if I got the chance!' Blue eyes flashed over the occupants of the room defiantly. 'Dane Carmichael was always bossing me around as if his family still owned this place!' she complained.

'You mean his family once lived on Kindyerra?' Janelle queried.

'Yes, it was the Carmichaels your father purchased the property from, or at least the Carmichael estate,' her mother began to explain. 'Apparently Dane's parents were killed in a level crossing accident when he was about fourteen, and he and his three younger brothers were put into the care of an aunt and uncle—he was Mrs Carmichael's brother, I believe—and it was he who sold Kindyerra to us. I understand he thought he could do better by the boys by investing the money, rather than attempting to run the property himself, because he had no farming experience at

all. Well, all four boys felt about Kindyerra much the same
as Ashley does, so during the weekends they used to come
out and give Ted a hand—they all knew him very well, of
course—and as each of them completed their schooling
they applied for work here. There was Dane and—and ...'
her forehead creased with her attempts to remember until
she looked enquiring at her son who supplied, 'Brent,' and
she went on with satisfaction, 'That's right, Brent! The
quiet one. Then Hal, who was next in line, was due to start
in about a month's time, but of course after that disastrous
encounter, Dane resigned ...'

'He was fired!' broke in Ashley heatedly.

'No, he wasn't! He'd resigned long before Dad ever
arrived home that day,' Lori was happily able to correct.

'Anyhow, to finish the story,' Ruth ignored their inter-
jections and started speaking again, 'Dane resigned, and
shortly afterwards Brent did too, and about six months or
so after that the whole family moved away from Willow
Bend and hasn't been back since.'

'So why couldn't they have left things that way? Why
did *he* have to come back now?' demanded Ashley stormily.
'Do you know, Lori?'

'Wouldn't have a clue,' that girl vetoed the suggestion
immediately. 'He certainly didn't mention anything about
why he was here while I was talking to him.'

'But even if he had, you probably wouldn't have heard
him anyway, because you would have been too busy moon-
ing over him like you used to,' Ashley couldn't resist the
mocking prod after her own period of embarrassment.

But as an extremely contented married woman, Lori
refused to be drawn. 'If I didn't have Alec, that might be a
distinct possibility,' she laughed. 'As every other girl in
town—bar you, of course—would readily admit, he was
gorgeous before. But now, with a bit more age,' she rolled
her eyes explicitly, 'he's devastating!'

Ashley muttered a dissident, 'Huh!' but Janelle ventured
a shy, 'Is he really that nice?' which had Lori stating, 'My
word!' in indisputable tones, and Alec taking part for the
first time with a laughing, 'Well, let's put it this way ...

None of the single men in town were too downhearted when the Carmichaels left. Why, even young Leigh, and he was only ... fifteen?' he sought and received corroboration from Bruce, 'had all the teenyboppers following him around wherever he went.'

'Conceited—all of them!' stated Ashley categorically, only to have Bruce moving his head just as emphatically in denial.

'No, they weren't! They just attracted females like honey does ants. Damn them!'

'Well, he'd better not set foot on Kindyerra again or there'll be trouble!' she took pleasure in informing him. 'Ralph's already told me he put Dane well and truly in his place once before, so I don't doubt he couldn't do the same again!'

Bruce and Alec exchanged broad grins. 'And if that's Ralph's story then we'd suggest he keeps it to himself, because we happened to be there the only time Ralph Skinner ever tried to pick Dane Carmichael in a fight, and we also know who came off worst from that set-to ... and it sure wasn't Dane!' Bruce relayed with obvious satisfaction.

'Oh!' Ashley didn't know whether to believe her brother or not, but decided that while Alec was there to back him up she wasn't likely to gain any satisfaction from following that line of thinking, so tried a completely different tack instead. 'I can't see why you're all so down on Ralph, anyway,' she criticised. 'Why should you two align yourselves with Dane against him?'

'It's obvious she wasn't at school at the same time we all were, isn't it?' quipped Alec, helping himself to another cup of coffee.

'And she had the nerve to call Dane a bully!' from Bruce.

Ashley frowned at them doubtfully, her blue eyes watchful. 'Are you implying that Ralph was something of a bully at school?' she queried in some uncertainty.

'You could say that,' Alec admitted dryly. 'Although I would have described him as a victimising predator myself. That's why it came as such a surprise to us all when he had a go at Dane that time, because Ralph usually preferred to only pick on those smaller and younger than himself! He seemed to think that just because his old man was one of the wealthiest in town, that gave him some sort of dictatorial rights over the rest of us.'

A horrified expression spread over Ashley's face and she turned to Bruce for support. 'He's having me on, isn't he?'

'Uh-uh! Sorry, little one, but that's the way it was. Ralph Skinner was the undisputed school bully!'

'Well, I'm blowed!'

The stunned look which clouded Ashley's eyes had them all laughing, and the mood for reminiscences was broken when Ruth made a move to begin the washing up and everyone left the table, but the unanticipated discovery stayed disquietingly in Ashley's mind long after Lori and Alec had left that evening.

Annoyingly it was still there the following night when, after they had attended a party at a friend's home, Ralph halted his brand new car in front of Lori and Alec's house.

'You've been pretty quiet all evening, Ashley,' he said, somewhat tartly it sounded to her. 'Anything wrong?'

'No, not really,' she sighed, and laid her head back against the cushioned upholstery, her eyes half closing. 'I'm sorry if I haven't been good company. I guess I'm more worried than I realised about the property.'

'But you're going to sell it! I would have thought your days of worrying over it were finished.'

Ashley's eyes did close now, tightly, as she willed herself not to get angry. It was always the same with Ralph. He never had been able to understand her desire to see Kindyerra making a profit again.

'And until it is sold, what would *you* suggest I do? Let the animals die of starvation?' she queried sarcastically before she could stop herself.

'There's no need to get smart,' he retorted peevishly. 'I don't know why you can't sell the damned things and be done with it! What's the point in flogging a dead horse, eh? I've been telling you for months that you should dispose of the place,' with undisguised gratification.

'Yes, well, your support in my hour of need is absolutely overwhelming, Ralph,' Ashley snapped, dragging herself upright and preparing to open the door. 'But now, if you'll excuse me, I'm tired, so I'll say goodnight and ...'

'Oh, hell, Ashley, don't let's argue,' Ralph groaned distractedly, and pulled her back against him, his hand cradling her head against his chest. 'You know how I feel about you, but I ...'

The rest of his pacifying words passed completely over Ashley's head because when he had pulled her against him so sharply she made a startling discovery. Ralph was becoming decidedly paunchy! And the revelation caught her so unawares that she was still cogitating over it when he regained her attention with a resentful, 'Ashley! You haven't been listening to a word I've said!'

'What?' She looked up with a frown, then, 'Oh, I'm sorry, Ralph, my mind must have been wandering. What were you saying?'

Ralph sighed and raked a hand through his light brown hair. 'It doesn't matter,' he told her in a deeply offended tone. 'I can see you're not interested.'

Curses! Now he was going into one of his rejected moods, and Ashley's eyes sought help from heaven at the thought. There had to be something she could say to snap him out of it, otherwise he would be just as likely to be in the same frame of mind when next she saw him, and the idea of that happening had her blurting out the first thing that came into her head.

'Did you know that Dane Carmichael was back in town?' she asked.

Evidently she couldn't have chanced upon anything better to rid Ralph of his air of dejection, for his light blue eyes fairly glittered when he sneered, 'Sure, I've seen him. He's still an arrogant bastard!'

'You've spoken to him, then,' she guessed.

Ralph snorted and confirmed it. 'But not for any longer than I had to, I can assure you!'

'And did he say how long he would be staying? Or—or why he's come back?'

'No, and I wasn't interested enough to ask!' His eyes narrowed suspiciously. 'What's it to you, anyway? You planning on chasing after him too like the rest of them?' he gibed.

Indignant that he should even consider her capable of such behaviour, Ashley rounded on him irritably. 'How ridiculous can you get? You should know by now what I think of Dane Carmichael—I've told you often enough.'

'That you have,' Ralph backed down almost contritely when he realised his mistake. 'It's just that nothing seems to have changed much. He's only been back two days and already he's collecting a female following—with that high and mighty little piece, Della Marchant, leading the parade,' he reported in disgust.

Ashley scowled and chewed at her bottom lip. 'He's still on the loose, then? He's not married?'

'It wouldn't seem like it. Unless, of course, he's left the little woman at home and is making the most out of his temporary freedom,' he suggested malevolently. 'But then any woman fool enough to marry someone like him would have to expect that, wouldn't she? He's not the type to accept the restrictions of marriage willingly.'

Wasn't he? Ashley found herself wondering how Ralph would know. He and Dane had never been friends, so he would hardly be in a position to speak from first-hand information, and although Ashley had definite opinions about the man herself, she had never been one to blindly believe someone else's assumptions regarding another's character.

In addition—an amused gleam appeared in her eyes—there had been just the tiniest hint of envy in Ralph's voice when he had spoken of Dane's female following, and his somewhat slighting reference to Della Marchant had Ashley speculating whether, at one time or another, he himself had made advances in that direction and received a contemptuous knock-back for his pains. Which, naturally, would be par for the course for Della! A neighbour of the Beaumonts, the tall disdainful redhead had always made it abundantly clear that when it came to the male company she kept it was her prerogative to do the choosing, and not vice versa.

So, all things considered, Ashley didn't judge it wise to become involved in a fruitless dissertation regarding either of them and, consequently, merely raised her shoulders a fraction to comment, 'Then it appears your original surmise was probably correct. He's still a bachelor,' with an indifferent intonation.

Whether or not he agreed, Ralph didn't bother to say, simply dismissing the matter with a jaundiced grimace and cupping her face within his two hands.

'How come we always end up talking about something or someone else other than us?' he charged impatiently. 'You're always so ready to discuss that damned property of yours, or whether wool prices are going up or coming down, or the price of machinery, or your sister's children, or even the weather! Anything but *us*!'

Ashley felt she could have been facetious and said she also tried to take an interest in the subjects which mattered most to him too, and that if he so obviously didn't care about what interested her, then why did he continue to see her? But as he apparently hadn't completely recovered from his earlier dejection, she decided to humour him and perhaps settle some of her own disquieting thoughts at the same time.

'All right, we'll talk about us,' she informed him calmly. 'Or you, if you prefer. What were you like as a child, Ralph?'

If she had slapped him he couldn't possibly have looked more astonished, and it was a few moments before he could expostulate, 'What in hell has that got to do with anything?'

'Very little, probably,' she allowed. 'I'm just curious, that's all.'

'About my childhood?'

'Why not? It all goes to make the sum total.'

'And it also conveniently saves talking about us, doesn't it?' His mouth thinned in anger as he let go of her abruptly. 'I'm only interested in the present, Ashley, not the past!'

'Without the past there can be no present—or future,'

she quoted levelly, and refusing to be deviated from her purpose.

'Meaning?' he demanded, suddenly watchful.

'Nothing in particular, except that I can't understand why you should be so annoyed with my asking,' she shrugged.

'Because there are other, more important questions I want you to ask me,' he revealed intensely. 'Like . . . where do I think would be a good place to spend our honeymoon? Where I think we should build our house and what style it should be? Even, what do I think our children will be like?'

He was rushing much too far ahead for Ashley's liking and she hastened to bring him back to the realities of the situation.

'But as I haven't yet said I *will* marry you, then I could hardly be expected to make any of those enquiries, could I?' she quizzed reasonably. 'And as to what any children we might have would be like—if we did marry, of course,' she hurried to add unless he thought it a foregone conclusion, 'then if you answered my first question we could well be on the way to knowing, couldn't we?'

'You're determined I'm going to reply to that damned silly query, aren't you?'

Ashley gave him an old-fashioned look, her blue eyes wide and innocent. 'If it's as silly as you make out, I fail to see why you're so determined not to.'

'Because there's nothing to tell, that's why!' Ralph bit out exasperatedly. 'I was an only child, but never a lonely one—because from an early age I learnt by my father's example that if you want something badly enough there's always more than one way to get it! School was okay—it didn't take me long to discover how to make that scene work for me—and afterwards, well, I joined the family building works and reached the top in record time.' He had the audacity to sound as if it was a monumental achievement instead of a matter of course. 'Now are you satisfied that you've finally heard the story of my childhood in half a dozen simple phrases?' he gibed.

Disappointed would have been more accurate, Ashley amended silently. It wasn't difficult to read between the lines and discover that Bruce and Alec had been telling the truth after all. Not that she had believed they would deliberately lie to her, but she had been hoping that they might somehow have been mistaken.

'So now can we get down to discussing us, and our plans?' Ralph demanded, and Ashley looked up into the heavily attractive face almost as if she was seeing him for the first time, suddenly noting the hard-lipped mouth, the pugnacious chin, the sharp eyes, and abruptly realising that she had never really regarded him so analytically before. However, what she was now seeing she didn't particularly like and she moved her head slowly, negatively, in response to his question.

'Some other time maybe, Ralph, hmm?' she sidestepped his intentions with a studied glance at the watch encircling her slender wrist. 'It's very late and I really should be going in. Friday is always one of our busiest days at the restaurant.'

'Now wait one minute!' he ejaculated furiously, gripping hold of her arm when she would have opened the car door. 'No one brushes me off after an evening out with a lame excuse like that, and least of all some bankrupt little bushie who doesn't know when someone's doing her a favour!'

Sheer contempt gave Ashley the strength to wrench out of his grasp and retaliate just as derisively, 'In that case, how about accepting it as a brush-off for good? Because this little bushie doesn't need a self-centred braggart to do her any favours, thanks all the same!' pushing the door open and swinging her legs to the ground.

'Don't be too sure of that!' he ground out after her in warning as she started to re-close the door. 'You just might find yourself regretting this in the months to come. Only don't expect me to take you back again, because when I drop a girl, she stays dropped!' he jeered.

Ashley bent down to look through the open window, a provoking smile dimpling soft cheeks. 'A fact which I'm sure must bring them no end of relief,' she mocked before spinning on her heel and marching for the gateway.

The scream of smoking tyres advised Ralph's departure before Ashley had even made it halfway up the path leading to the front door. Perhaps Lori had been correct, she mused ironically. Things had been cooling off between herself and Ralph, and it had only needed tonight's altercation to send them into a deep freeze altogether.

CHAPTER THREE

ON reaching the high side of Stony Gully, Ashley reined in beneath a gracefully weeping belah and eased forward in the saddle, the black dog which had been trotting along beside her making the most of this unexpected halt by squatting near the base of the tree, his tongue drooping moistly from the side of his mouth. Apart from the three or four ewes at the far end of the depression there didn't appear to be any other sheep in this particular area to muster towards the mob which Ted was slowly driving towards the corner gates for dispersal into the high paddock, and Ashley took the opportunity to gaze out over the panorama spread below her. This had always been her favourite view of Kindyerra, where after good rains the grass recovered almost overnight to become a rolling green carpet over the gentle slopes, and the trees flourished with new vigour within a smoky blue heat haze which would shimmer invitingly across the burgeoning land. Today, only a fine film of red dust hovered insubstantially above the parched and cracking earth, while the searing heat of the sun overhead beat down relentlessly and reflected back from the bare soil with an eye-burning glare.

Sighing at the depressing vision the scene now afforded, Ashley urged Amarina forward, preparing to descend into the gully, when a sudden movement away to the north attracted her attention and she stopped once more, her gaze narrowing curiously.

Far in the distance, on Billambang—the property owned by the Marchants which bounded Kindyerra in that direction—she could just make out what appeared to be three riders moving at a casual gait towards the fence which separated the two stations. She knew it wasn't Della because that girl always rode a distinctive palomino, and it wasn't her father, Ramsay, either as he was normally mounted on a big roan, while these three men—they were close enough now to be able to distinguish that much about them—were riding a pair of chestnuts and a bay. They weren't city-bred riders either, she ascertained subconsciously, because they sat too still and easy in the saddle for that.

Then who were they? she frowned interestedly. They would surely have heard if the Marchants had guests staying with them—new faces always made welcome news in this part of the world—and if they had been surely Della or her father would have accompanied them in order to make sure they didn't become lost. Not that these three appeared to be in need of any guidance, she noted, because they seemed to know exactly where they were going and there was no hesitation as to which was the best way to take them there. Were they hunters, then, out after the wild pigs in the drying marshes? If they were, it was an unusual route they were using to reach them.

With a wry smile she shook her head to dismiss the inquisitive thoughts and heeled Amarina out into the sunlight. Whoever they were, they weren't doing any harm, and she didn't have the time to sit here all morning speculating as to the reason for their presence. With a low whistle for Flash to follow her, Ashley tightened her grip on the reins and started down the steep incline, one last considering glance being directed northwards before she dropped completely out of sight.

Oh, no! Her immediate thought was one of dismay that roos must have brought down a section of the fence again, because that hurried look had shown the first of the riders to be walking his horse calmly on to Kindyerra when there should have been several strands of wire to bar his entry, and her second was that she had better ride that way in order to tell them they were now inadvertently trespassing.

At the bottom of the gully she wheeled the mare to the left and pressed her into a canter, following what had once been an ancient watercourse for about half a mile until it petered out, then winding her way between the trees to where one of the riders was stationary beside a stand of eucalypts. Of the other two there was no sign and Ashley cast a nervous glance about her as she drew closer. If they were here after game, she hoped they *were* hunters as she had first presumed, and not just shooters! The latter kind weren't always particular about their target, their main criterion seeming to be, 'If it moves, shoot it,' and she had no wish for either Amarina or herself to become a victim of their thoughtlessness as had many another grazier's valuable stock in the past.

The man's head was shaded by a stockman's hat as he bent to light a cigarette so that Ashley couldn't discern his features when she eased the mare into a walk for the last few yards. The only observations that she could make being that he was tall and broad-shouldered, and that the fawn drill of his pants was stretched tightly about the hard muscles of his long legs.

'I'm sorry,' she called out pleasantly. 'You probably didn't realise it, but when you came through that fence you crossed on to . . .'

'Well, well, well! If it isn't the little brat Beaumont!' a deeply sardonic voice interposed in a lazy drawl as mocking green eyes lifted to her stunned face to send disturbing prickles down her spine and have her reefing Amarina unusually severely to a stop.

It took her only a few moments to run a watchful scrutiny over that familiar face. To see for herself that what Lori had said was true. Even as a child she had realised that Dane Carmichael was good-looking, but now, with the rounded edges planed into decisive sharpness, and coupled with that dark curling hair, the sea green eyes, well shaped nose and firmly moulded mouth, he was both a stimulating challenge as well as a warning, and Ashley could feel her nerves contracting involuntarily at the thought.

As if this unexpected knowledge was all she had been waiting for, the childish resentment she had harboured all through the years now flared into a fully mature antagonism she was as unable to control, and not to be outdone by his satirical greeting she swallowed hard and rested one hand on her hip, her eyes holding his defiantly, her whole attitude one of provocation.

'Well, well! If it isn't the scourge of the juveniles!' she gibed in turn. 'Been chastising many twelve-year-olds of late, Dane?' with one slim eyebrow arching enquiringly.

The sound of his deep laughter hung heavily in the still air between them as he shook his head to deny aggravatingly, 'Uh-uh! I only ever found one who needed it.'

Ashley tut-tutted in mock consolation. 'How disappointing for you! Just think of all that dormant energy and skill going to waste.'

The wide mouth quirked consideringly. 'Well, maybe now that I'm back in Willow Bend it won't for much longer,' he remarked with obvious meaning as he casually studied the glowing tip of his cigarette. 'You don't appear to have changed at all—you're still the pert little brat you always were!'

'While you're still the same high-handed brute!' she threw back at him contemptuously, blue eyes sparkling brightly within their dark lashes. 'But let me give you a word of warning, Dane ...' She lowered her voice to one of intense sincerity. 'If you ever lay a hand on me again, so help me, I'll do what my father only threatened ... I'll take a stockwhip to you!'

Dane ground out his cigarette unhurriedly on the sole of his boot, almost as if he hadn't heard her, then his right arm snaked out so rapidly that Ashley couldn't avoid it and instead found her wrist gripped by long fingers with a steely strength.

'And that piece of bluffing bravado is just as amusing as it was when he uttered it,' he informed her with cool derision. 'Your father never even owned a stockwhip, let alone knew how to use one, and although you may consider yourself a little more proficient, I wouldn't recommend you ever attempt anything so foolhardy as what you've just suggested. You may have grown up, Ashley,' even white teeth gleamed in an appreciative smile as his eyes ranged appraisingly over her curving form, 'but you're still not quite big enough to challenge me to a show of strength, so don't ever be persuaded into thinking you are!'

'Then let go of my arm!' she demanded heatedly, fighting against his remorseless grip and the steady thumping of her heart as a result of that unexpected smile. 'And get off Kindyerra too! You're not wanted here, and—and you're trespassing!'

'Now fancy that—who would have thought it!' he taunted mockingly, his gaze straying pointedly back to the gaping hole in the fence, but still giving no indication as to when he would release his hold. 'If that's the best you can do by the property I'm not surprised you have people intruding. Although in my case,' he gave her such a tormenting look that Ashley could cheerfully have hit him, 'I'm afraid you have the bull by the tail as usual, because your mother was most welcoming when I spoke to her on the phone earlier this morning and invited us to call in when she found out we'd be coming this way. And your mother *is* the legal owner of Kindyerra now, isn't she, brat?'

Ashley was only too well aware what he was trying to imply—that she had no right to order him from the property in the circumstances—and the fact that he was legally correct wasn't making it any easier to accept her mother's defection in suggesting he call when she knew very well that Ashley didn't want him there at any price!

Now she answered his query with a disgruntled, 'As you very well know!' and a suspicious, 'But just who are the other two with you anyway? I don't want them causing trouble,' as she looked from side to side in a futile effort to locate them.

'Don't worry, they won't,' she was assured complacently. 'They're just checking out the rest of the fence for you. From the look of the place we thought it more than likely that this break wasn't the only one.'

As she sensed some criticism for her handling of the property, Ashley's temper rose and a flush covered her cheekbones. 'We've been doing our best, but we have had a drought for the last three years, you know—in case that fact has escaped your notice!' she mocked aggressively.

'Unfortunately, it apparently wasn't enough,' he commented ironically, and at Ashley's puzzled creasing of her forehead, 'Your best,' which had her reaching out with her free hand to hit at his bronzed forearm, but with an infuriating laugh he finally set her at liberty and moved agilely out of range.

While she was still able, Ashley gathered up the reins again and swung Amarina's head around. 'Well, even though my poor efforts may not come up to your expectations, I do still have work to do, so . . .' she touched a finger to the brim of her hat and gave him a smile as taunting as any of his own had been, 'I can't say it's been a pleasure to see you again, because it hasn't! Instead, I'll just wish you a speedy trip back to where you came from!' as the mare began to increase her stride.

'Exactly what I was hoping myself,' he called after her in ringing tones, and to her amazement she found the idea that he would be as pleased to leave Willow Bend again as she would be to see him go vaguely discomfiting.

She wasn't given any time to dwell on the matter, however, as the rest of the day was occupied with the depressing task of mustering the pathetically weakened sheep into another paddock where Ted had previously been able to distribute some fodder. Not that there was much of it, but at least it was better than what they'd had.

At three o'clock they stopped in order to give them all a spell from the choking dust which they had been breathing. The sheep either stood or sank wearily to the ground where they came to rest and the dogs, with no guarding to do, came to lie gratefully beneath the trees and share a little of the iced water Ashley and Ted had brought with them in containers. The first mouthful was used solely to rinse the dust away, but the next was like pure nectar as it slid shiveringly down parched throats, and Ashley licked at her lips in pleasure before her worried gaze returned to the pitiful mob huddled together among some bushes a short distance away.

'We almost made it, Ted,' she broke their companionable silence dismally, recollecting how optimistic they had been before the drought descended, when after four years of stringent budgeting and careful planning it looked as if they were going to succeed after all in repaying their debts. 'If only we'd had one more good year before this happened we might have been able to afford to send the majority of the stock away on agistment like the Marchants did.' She sighed and pressed her lips together tightly. 'I was only looking across at Billambang this morning from the ridge and they've got a faint covering of green in some patches where the grass has had a chance to grow after that last light shower they had.'

Ted's work-worn hand felt for and clasped hers sympathetically. 'We tried, little missie, we tried, and it wasn't as if we didn't know how big a task we were attempting, for there were enough warnings and cautions given after your father died,' he reminded her slowly.

'I guess so,' Ashley accepted his reasoning reluctantly. 'It's just so hard to think that it's all been for nothing, and if we *do* move from here,' her eyes closing with repugnance at the thought, 'what am I going to do in town? Be a waitress all my life while trying to convert some tiny quarter acre building block into a sheep station? I'll go stark, raving mad—I'm sure I will!' she groaned despairingly.

'Perhaps the new owner when he comes will wish to employ someone who knows the property well.'

Ashley didn't hold out much hope of this happening. 'I doubt it,' she shrugged. 'After all, you said yourself that from here on Kindyerra needs stronger backs than yours or mine, and Dane Carmichael didn't seem to think we'd done such a good job when I saw him this morning,' morosely.

Coal black eyes swung to meet hers quickly. 'You saw Dane?' he questioned intently, and after her brooding, 'Mmm,' he wanted to know, 'What did he have to say?'

'Nothing much,' she admitted sourly. 'It was mainly a continuation of his normal sarcasms. He reckons I'm still a brat,' with a flippant kind of resentment.

'And were you?'

Suddenly she laughed. 'Trust you to ask something like that! But if I was, it was only because he started by calling me one before I even realised who I was talking to. Anyway, what does it matter what he thinks? I gather he's not planning to stay around for long, so I don't expect we'll meet again ... thank heavens!'

'He actually said he wouldn't be staying?'

'Something to that effect,' she relayed happily, then turned to look at him closely. 'Why? Did you want to see him?'

'I already have,' he replied quietly. 'As well as Hal and Leigh.'

Ashley almost choked on the water she was in the act of swallowing and stared at him dumbfounded, until she regained her wits and exploded into a welter of enquiries.

'When did you see him? Why didn't you tell me?' And before he could even open his mouth to attempt a reply, 'Is that who was with him earlier—Hal and Leigh? I wouldn't have minded seeing them, they were always easy to get along with! What are they like now? Are they married?'

'One at a time, little missie, and all in good time,' Ted impressed on her with a wide grin splitting his face, laughing at her impatience. 'You seem very anxious to hear about the rest of the family.'

'Stop beating about the bush, Ted,' he was urged with a responsive smile. 'You know very well that you're as keen to tell me as I am to listen.'

'Okay, Ashley, I won't tease you any more,' he chuckled. 'I met up with them this morning while you were out looking for stragglers and I was keeping the others on the move. They came part of the way from the Marchants' along the fence, and the reason I didn't mention it was because I thought it best not to.' His head tilted sideways and a wry look entered his eyes. 'You're not usually very eager to hear the Carmichael name mentioned.' A steady look in return from Ashley and he continued, 'As for Hal and Leigh ... they're much as they always were, and interested to hear what's been happening on the property since they left the area. As for whether they're married ...' he hunched his shoulders vaguely, 'they didn't say.'

After digesting this information thoughtfully for a few seconds, Ashley had to ask in some surprise, 'Didn't Dane ask about Kindyerra too?' Considering his remarks to her, she would have thought it extremely likely, but Ted began shaking his head.

'No, we spoke about many things but, apart from saying it looked as if we'd been hit very hard by the drought, that was the only time he mentioned it.'

Which had probably been another slighting condemnation for her management, Ashley decided mutinously, but she still couldn't let the matter settle in her mind.

'But doesn't that strike you as strange?' she asked. 'Especially when we know how much Dane used to think of it.'

Ted took a long draught of his drink and wiped his mouth with the back of his hand. 'Maybe he had other things on his mind. I gather they have a number of business interests which take up their time and thought these days.'

'Then why are they here in Willow Bend?' Ashley pounced, the creases furrowing her forehead put there by inquisitive puzzlement. 'And—and where did they get the money for all these so-called business interests? I knew they weren't exactly on the breadline when they lived here, but I didn't know they were that well off,' she frowned.

'You're forgetting that, although the uncle who took them in when their parents died might not have known anything about station management, he was a very capable businessman, and I believe the money from the sale of Kindyerra which he invested for them made a very nice profit,' he informed her knowledgeably. 'Also, from what they were saying, I gather that at some time or another mineral mining has had a fair share in their success too.'

'So they've been steadily climbing up while we've been slowly, but surely, going down,' Ashley pondered quietly, more to herself than to Ted, and abruptly finding the implication annoying although she couldn't have explained just why that should be so. She wasn't normally an envious person, but somehow that last disclosure had rankled.

Determinedly pushing her vexations aside, she returned to the question which still niggled. 'But you still haven't answered as to why they're back in Willow Bend.'

'Perhaps for no other reason than to renew old friendships,' he offered indifferently. 'The family was always well liked and respected, you know.'

'And very much so by the Marchants!' Ashley retorted with a mocking asperity. 'Is that where they're staying? So dear Della can keep the field all to herself?'

'You sound a little jealous when you say that,' he teased rashly.

Ashley came upright from her leaning position against the trunk of a tree so fast that her hat fell off. 'That's the most idiotic thing I've ever heard you say!' she flared indignantly, clamping her headgear savagely back in place. 'I wouldn't have Dane Carmichael staying at our place if you paid me . . . and you know it!'

'You didn't find him attractive?'

Blue eyes rose skywards and she expelled a heavy breath ironically. 'Oh, of course I did!' she assented in a rare moment of honesty where the subject of their discussion was concerned. 'Besides, you would have accused me of either being as blind as a bat, or as sour as a lemon, If I'd said anything different,' she added dryly. 'But it doesn't mean I like him any better than I ever did! And as for the other—well, I only meant that the gossip flying around town has Della in the forefront of those making a play for you know who!'

Ted's eyes looked faintly reproving. 'I didn't think you listened to gossip.'

'I don't usually,' she returned quickly, a colourful stain of discomfort covering her honey-coloured skin. 'But it's hard not to when it's such common knowledge. On Friday, I think every customer who came into the restaurant got around to talking about them over one course or another,' she defended herself.

'You've been eavesdropping too?' he quizzed in a joking manner, only Ashley wasn't in the mood to take it that way and jumped to her feet irritably.

'No, I wasn't,' she denied tensely, brushing her jeans

down with unnecessary force. 'It's not my fault if they keep me waiting to take their orders while they finish their conversations.' A sudden wry smile lightened her expression. 'My thoughts might be out here most of the time ... but my ears certainly aren't!'

By Wednesday morning the household was in an uproar and even Ashley wasn't completely immune to the unlimited buoyancy the other members of her family were displaying.

Jack Prescott had rung her mother the previous Monday to advise that he had fortunately been successful in locating their prospective buyer and that the gentleman was prepared to make the journey to Willow Bend in order to discuss the matter with her. Could she make herself available at his office on Wednesday afternoon at four o'clock, together with the relevant books of accounts, stock records, etcetera? The answer had, of course, been an unequivocal, 'Yes,' and from then on speculation and anticipation had been rife.

By the time Ruth was due to leave to keep her appointment, her face was flushed and when she came across to where Ashley was waiting for Tony to fill her next order for the restaurant's dining room she was becoming quite nervous.

'Stop worrying yourself into a cold sweat, Mum,' she was ordered with a smile and an encouraging wink which hid Ashley's true feelings well. 'If he offers you a good deal ... grab it!'

'Oh, Ashley!' Ruth hugged her daughter convulsively. 'It would be such a weight off my mind.' Then, doubtfully, 'But what if it isn't? A good deal, I mean.'

Ashley's reply was a straightforward and incisive, 'Then don't accept!' but with the afterthought, 'although Jack would be the best person to advise you on that score. Just remember, there's always other fish in the sea—even if they aren't as eager as this one seems to be to take the bait.'

'But what would we do in the meantime?' her mother queried worriedly. 'After your comments regarding the state of the stock last weekend . . . what can we do?'

'Nothing much,' Ashley responded with a blitheness she certainly wasn't feeling. 'We can't take them into the sale-yards because the price they'd bring wouldn't even cover the cost of the freight, and at the moment extra expenses like that we don't need! So I suppose we just carry on as best we can or, who knows, it may even rain,' she laughed hollowly.

'But . . .'

'No "buts",' Ashley shook her head firmly and glanced towards the wall clock over the swinging doors which led into the restaurant. 'And you'd better get a move on or you'll be late. We'll pick you up when you've finished . . . okay?'

On her way to the back door, Ruth turned about sharply. 'Oh, no, that's all right, you don't have to wait. I forgot to mention it, but Jack said he would be able to give me a lift home because he has to go out to the Yeldhams' place tonight anyway,' she named a family whose property was only some ten miles away from their own. 'No, you three go on home and have your dinner with Lori and Alec. I could be quite late.'

'You're sure you wouldn't rather we waited?'

Ruth waved the suggestion aside with one slightly agitated hand. 'No, thank you, love, I'll be all right, and I'll —I'll let you know everything that happens when I arrive home.'

'Okay, if that's the way you want it,' Ashley smiled. 'At least with it being Wednesday you'll only have to tell it once, there won't be any need for repeats with Lori and Alec already on the scene.'

'No, that's something,' her mother smiled in agreement, and with one last half wave departed while she still had time to reach Jack's office before four.

Dinner that evening was a period of partly asked questions and partly finished answers while Ruth's children awaited her return. Everyone, excepting Ashley to some degree, was secretly hopeful of the outcome, but no one really dared to bring their aspirations out into the open.

Ashley suspected this had been brought about in the main through their deference for her sentiments regarding the property, but during the last ten days she had unwillingly, but increasingly, become aware that there was really very little alternative left to them but to sell. The distressing work she and Ted had undertaken last weekend had been enough to finally convince her of that.

The sun had well and truly set and they were all watching television—or, at least, they were all looking in that direction—when the sound of an approaching vehicle had them all sitting forward on the edge of their seats, and it was a unanimous decision which elected Bruce to go out on to the verandah to meet Ruth and pass on the family's greetings to Jack Prescott instead of them all traipsing out there like Brown's cows.

It seemed an age to Ashley before they heard Jack calling his goodbyes and the noise of his car receding into the distance. A lifetime in which she sat back and then forward again on her chair, twined her fingers together nervously, and crossed and uncrossed her legs continuously. But now that her mother was actually entering the room she discovered she was holding her breath as the practical side of Lori's nature asserted itself and she asked considerately, 'Would you like dinner first—or a cup of tea?'

Mrs Beaumont sank down into one of the worn armchairs and replied, 'A cup of tea, thanks, dear,' with a grateful sigh as she happily took in the expectant faces surrounding her.

Ashley let out her breath slowly, half in relief and half in sorrow. It was done—a *fait accompli*! Kindyerra was sold! Or at least in the process thereof, she amended silently. The radiant expression in her mother's eyes told her all she wanted to know. The questions regarding the finer details of the transaction she would leave to the others in an effort to give herself time to become accustomed to the idea—if that was possible.

Janelle could hardly wait, though, until Lori returned with the promised tea before she loosed her first excited enquiry. 'Well, what happened, Mum? Is he going to buy it?' she came straight to the point.

Ruth surveyed the anxious faces turned her way one by one, two sympathetic creases appearing between her brows when she came to her second daughter's stiffly controlled features, and then her eyes passed on and she couldn't contain her happiness any longer.

'Yes! Yes, he is,' she divulged animatedly, and had to wait for the general rejoicing to die down before she could continue with, 'and a deposit has already been paid to Jack, so there's little fear of the sale not going ahead.'

'It really is all settled, then? You've signed a contract?' quizzed Alec, and received a spirited nod of affirmation in response.

Bruce was the next with a query. 'Was the price a good one?' he probed warily.

'Better than I'd hoped for,' his mother smiled her delight and named an amount which immediately brought forth more expressions of jubilation.

'But after the mortgages are paid and all debts and expenses cleared, will there be enough left to buy yourself a house somewhere?' Bruce gave voice to his deepest concern.

'Jack thinks so ... just!' Ruth laughed lightly and took a sip of her tea. 'Although there won't be any need to worry about that aspect for a while because there was a—a proviso added to the contract which sort of—sort of covers that,' she finished not quite so lightly.

'Proviso?' Lori frowned, while Bruce demanded, 'What sort of proviso?'

Ruth shook her head urgently. 'Nothing terrible, I can assure you! Just the opposite, in fact!' she was quick to allay their suspicions. 'It only concerns Ashley and myself really.'

As she heard this Ashley's eyes narrowed in puzzlement and she at last joined the conversation to query cautiously, 'In what way?'

'Only that we agree to stay on here for at least six months after the sale is finalised in order to help with the changeover,' her mother explained elatedly at having been able to give them all some good news.

To stay for another six months, of course she agreed—unreservedly—and Ashley said as much aloud, the tension suddenly leaving her body and giving her something to look forward to.

'That's marvellous,' Ruth sighed contentedly. 'I thought you'd be pleased.'

'But what about Bruce and me?' Janelle broke in dolefully. 'Where are we going to live?'

Mrs Beaumont laughed at the mournful look on her youngest child's face and assured her not to worry because, 'That's all been taken care of too. Once the circumstances had been explained, it was readily agreed that both of you should be allowed to remain on the property until either I leave, or you make other arrangements for yourselves in the meantime if you so wish.'

'Oh, that's all right, then,' conceded Janelle, slightly mollified now that the conditions had been made clear. But then her head tilted consideringly and she wanted to be told, 'Just who is this white knight who's saved us from the debtors' court, or whatever?'

'I—er——' Ruth fidgeted in her chair and looked decidedly uncomfortable. 'Actually, it's a—a company, dear,' she eventually disclosed, albeit somewhat faintly.

'Oh!' exclaimed Bruce interestedly. 'What's their name?'

'I'm—it's—I doubt if you would—um—know their name, Bruce. I believe they're registered in Queensland, and—and . . .'

'Heavens, the excitement must have been too much for you, Mum. You've gone all stuttery,' Lori interrupted with a grin, while Ashley inserted a helpful, 'If they're a rural concern I might know of them. I read all the country papers.'

'That's right,' Bruce endorsed emphatically. 'Ash would probably know. What did you say their name was?'

Ruth took another mouthful of tea, placed her cup on a nearby table, and clasped her hands together in her lap. 'I—I didn't say, dear,' she murmured uneasily, 'but it happens to be ...' she took a deep breath and burst out, 'Carmichael Investments.'

Momentarily it would have been possible to hear the proverbial pin drop, so absolute was the silence which followed this bombshell, then, as each of them had mentally predicted, it was Ashley who took over the questioning.

'*Who* did you say?' came the low seething request for clarification.

'I said—Carmichael Investments,' her mother repeated tautly. 'It's owned by—by Dane and his brothers.'

'And you signed a contract with *him*!' Ashley gasped in disbelief. 'A contract, moreover, giving an undertaking that we would stay here while he takes over! Mum! How could you?'

'Because it was too good an offer to refuse in Jack's estimation,' Ruth answered a little more calmly now that the worst was over. 'And I thought it would make it easier for you if you had another six months in which to get used to the idea of our leaving.'

It would have done had anyone else been the buyer, Ashley mutely agreed, but not all of her queries had been answered yet. 'Okay, I can understand that, but now what I would really like to know is ...' Her eyes darkened suspiciously. 'What were his reasons for suggesting such a condition? What's he going to gain out of all this sudden philanthropy?'

'It certainly wasn't philanthropy which prompted that stipulation, dear,' Ruth protested hurriedly. 'Dane was saying he very much needs someone to keep the homestead running smoothly for him, and someone who knows the property well to bring the books up to date and to fill him in on various aspects of management which have taken place since he left.'

'The lying hypocrite!' Ashley blazed uncontrollably, her nails digging into her hands as her fingers curled with the force of her feelings. 'Oh, I don't doubt he wants someone to run the homestead, but he certainly doesn't need *me* for the other! He knows this property as well as I do— probably better,' with a galling look of mortification at the admission, 'and if he bothered to look for them he'd be able to see for himself the "various aspects of management which have taken place since he left",' she mimicked sarcastically. 'No, the only reason Dane Carmichael wants me here is so he can gloat about having got Kindyerra back again—which no doubt is what he always intended—and to pay me back for all those things I said to him years ago!'

Bruce started to chuckle and a wide grin pulled at his mouth. 'Ashley, love, you sound as if you're becoming a trifle paranoic. Dane's buying the place as a business venture, not as a means of retribution,' he laughed at her mistrusting expression. 'You're letting your disappointment at having to sell cloud your reasoning. I don't suppose he even remembers the precocious things you used to come out with, let alone intends avenging them . . . he's just not that type!'

Ashley wasn't convinced. 'Huh! Little you know!' she retorted mockingly. 'Believe me, our little feud is quite mutual . . . he dislikes me just as much as I dislike him!'

With another grin to match Lori's broadening one, Bruce threw up his hands in surrender as his mother began to speak.

'But, Ashley dear, if you're going to be working for Dane, don't you think . . .'

'Who said anything about working for him?' she was cut off swiftly. 'You only said the agreement was that we should stay on here.'

'Well, of course, that meant we would be working for him—that was the arrangement,' Ruth exclaimed. 'We couldn't afford to give up our jobs in town without replacing those lost salaries with something.'

This was a rationalisation Ashley couldn't dispute, but she wasn't about to put herself in bondage in order to support it. 'In that case, you can count me out straight away!' she told her parent categorically. 'I may have been able to survive six months of his company if I'd been a free agent, but being answerable to him for that length of time . . . no, thank you! . . . I'd rather keep working at the restaurant!'

which showed just how strongly she felt about the matter.

'But you can't do that, can you, Ashley?' broke in Janelle enquiringly. 'Not after Mum's already agreed to the condition.'

'You wait and see if I can't!' came the dogmatic return. 'Mum may have signed on my behalf, but I certainly didn't! —so our wily friend might find he hasn't been so clever as he imagined, after all!'

Lori now sat forward quickly and scolded, 'That's not the point, Ashley. The fact is, Mum has given her word, and up until now the members of this family have always honoured their word!'

'Which is probably exactly what he was depending on!' Ashley pointed out acidly as she swung out of her chair and walked to the door. 'Now, having got all that settled, if you'll excuse me, I feel the need for some action, so I'll just take myself off for a ride.'

Janelle looked up at her, round-eyed. 'You can't! It's dark outside.'

A despairing shake of her head and Ashley gave her a somewhat patronising look. 'It is not dark outside,' she corrected evenly. 'There happens to be a full moon and that makes it possible to see almost as well as in daylight.'

'But Dane's coming over soon—I invited him,' her mother called after her agitatedly. 'What shall I say when you're not here?'

Ashley turned back, her eyes gleaming, her lips curving. 'I don't expect you'll have to say anything ... he'll get the message!' she smiled pleasurably at the thought, whirling out of the room and leaving the ensuing sound of mixed voices behind her.

CHAPTER FOUR

HAVING changed into a pair of pale faded jeans and a coloured shirt, Ashley ambled slowly over to the horse yard, drinking in the cool air after the heat of the day, and gazing up at the clear evening sky where a myriad stars twinkled and glittered vividly.

For a moment she stopped and looked consideringly in the direction of Ted and Neillie's cottage, then sighed and dismissed the idea. No, it wasn't more conversation she needed to discharge this feeling of tension which had enveloped her ever since learning the identity of Kindyerra's purchaser. Slowly she moved on, retrieving a bridle from one of the sheds as she passed, and eventually reaching the paddock where Amarina and the two other station horses were to be found.

She pulled herself up on to the second wooden rail and prepared to give the mare a low whistle, but the sound which issued from her throat was a muffled squeal of surprise when two hands spanned her slender waist and deposited her back on the ground again and a deep voice demanded,

'Where do you think you're going at this time of night?'

A second to recover from the shock and to regain a little of her composure, and then Ashley spun around, her eyes widely challenging his right to ask. 'I don't think that's any of your business,' she smiled deliberately into Dane's shadowed face, then mocked, 'I wouldn't dream of questioning you as to why you chose to ride over instead of driving,' on seeing the familiar chestnut tied to the fence further along the yard.

Strong white teeth gleamed in the bronzed darkness of his face and his head inclined sideways. 'Did your mother tell you?'

Determined to show as little of what she was feeling as

she could, Ashley replied as casually as possible. 'That you're the one who's buying Kindyerra? Yes, she told us.'

'And is that all you have to say on the subject?' he drawled, baitingly to Ashley's ears, and she could feel her resentment growing.

'Why? What did you expect me to say, Dane?' she quizzed defiantly. 'That I was shocked to find you were the so mysterious buyer that Jack had in mind? Well, you made sure of that with all your secrecy, didn't you?' she answered her own question bitterly. 'Or that I would have preferred to see anyone other than you buy the place? I'm sure you knew that anyway! Or maybe you were only interested to hear how I'd railed at your cunning little proviso?' she threw at him witheringly. 'Well, I have news for you! I'm afraid you miscalculated on that one! You see, I haven't the slightest intention in the world of working for you for six months, so you can take your condition and go jump in the damned lake with it! I didn't agree to it!'

'Your mother did on your behalf,' he said coolly.

'So? Sue me!' she invited tauntingly.

'There wouldn't be any point in it,' he advised ironically, hands thrusting into the back pockets of his moleskin pants. 'Your whole family will be bankrupt if the sale doesn't go through and that mortgage of yours is called in.'

Confidently, Ashley's chin angled a little higher. 'You're hoping for a bit much, aren't you?' she scoffed. 'Why should the mortgage be called in just because the sale falls through?'

'Because I shall make sure that it is.'

'How?' in utter disbelief.

'Simply by telling my solicitor to make out the appropriate forms in order to do so,' he retorted dryly. 'You see, I happen to be your mortgagee.'

'You're lying!' The words burst from Ashley's lips before he had even finished the last word. 'The name on all the documents is that of George Pike.'

'Said solicitor—and my agent. You didn't really think I'd let you know I was actually the mortgagee, did you?'

The confidence which had been boosting Ashley such a

short time earlier now sagged defeatedly and she bit at her lip in consternation. 'And—and if I don't comply with this stipulation of yours, you'll call in the mortgage, is that it?'

Upon the totally unyielding, and unfeeling, nod of agreement she received in response, Ashley's breathing deepened wrathfully. 'You really are an unprincipled louse, aren't you?' she denounced sarcastically. 'You've always meant to take Kindyerra away from us!' completely forgetting how thankful she had been on each occasion when Jack had managed to gain an extension on the time period for the repayment of their loans.

'I also gave you enough chances to make something out of it,' Dane snapped icily as his eyes gave a quick and pointed scrutiny to the dilapidated sheds and collapsing yards. 'Looks like you did a real good job,' he jeered disparagingly.

As if discovering there was no way to circumvent his proviso hadn't been enough, now she was also having to endure his deprecatory remarks concerning all the back-breaking work she had put in over the years and unbidden tears burned at the back of her eyes at the unfairness of it all.

'Oh! You—you . . .!' she began, then turned her back on him hurriedly, her trembling fingers surreptitiously brushing away the moisture from her lashes lest he should see, her head downbent.

Dane gazed at the slim figure before him, the blonde hair turning to glistening gold in the moonlight, and ran a hand exasperatedly around the back of his neck.

'Then stop trying to draw blood every time we meet, honey,' he advised with a sigh, his hand now reaching out and coming to rest on the vulnerable nape of her neck. 'You'll be the one to suffer most if you rile me too often.'

The touch of his hand on her skin had Ashley growing warm from her head down to her toes, and the rate of her pulse increasing dramatically. Annoyed by her own adolescent reaction, she directed her anger towards the person she blamed for all her new problems.

'Oh, leave me alone, Dane! Just leave me alone!' she

ordered tersely, and pulled away from that disturbing hand. 'You've successfully managed to take away my home and everything else I've ever worked for! Made sure I have no option but to suffer your disparaging and/or gloating comments for the next half year, and implied that I've let the place go to rack and ruin! Isn't that enough? Are you now suggesting I give up my right of free speech too?' she gibed belligerently.

Even in the dusky light she could see those green eyes of his dancing with laughter. 'Would you . . . if I asked?' he goaded deliberately, and Ashley was too incensed to do anything but retaliate furiously.

'Go to blazes! I'd rather lose Kindyerra twice over than do anything *you* ask!' she lashed back at him. 'Believe me, I'll be riling you at every opportunity which presents itself!'

'Okay, as long as you have no complaints when I do the same in return!' Dane countered roughly, broad shoulders flexing, and took her completely unawares when a long-fingered hand caught hold of her arm and swung her up against a hard-muscled chest. 'It seems such a pity to let all that fervent emotion go to waste,' was his next derisive taunt as one arm slid inescapably around her and a hand came up to span her jaw.

Ashley struggled violently as the firm curving mouth closed inexorably with hers, the initial searing contact with its vibrant power of domination sending the blood rioting through her veins even as she continued straining to be free. But slowly, the pressure of his lips changed, lessening slightly to tease instead of master, and Ashley could feel her defences crumbling waywardly beneath this new persuasion which tantalised and attracted to such an extent that she was totally oblivious to her struggles finally ceasing, and she began to return his kisses with an ardour which recklessly invited a more sensuous exploration.

Only when Dane's mouth lifted from hers to glide provocatively down the side of her neck to the hectic pulse drumming at the base of her throat did her mind make another stand for resistance and she collected her senses with a humiliated gasp for her actions, her pliant form suddenly becoming rigid and unyielding as she wrenched herself frantically out of his hold.

'How dare you!' she hurled at him with all the indignation she could muster. 'You needn't think that by exercising your masculine virility you're going to keep me in subjection!' Which was quite a difficult statement to make convincingly in view of her recent willing surrender, and her face reddened with embarrassment under the sardonic gaze she was awarded in return, but she pressed on as resolutely as possible.

'And now, if you don't mind . . .' her tone indicating quite clearly that she didn't care whether he did or not, 'I'm going for a ride as I originally planned! The rest of them,' a waving hand signified the homestead as she brushed past him haughtily and clambered on to the yard rail again, 'are all waiting with open arms to welcome the conquering hero, I'm sure you'll be thrilled to know!'

'You're not going anywhere tonight!' was the arbitrary contradiction which accompanied his lifting her down once more and tossing her discarded bridle over the nearest gate-post. 'It's you I mainly wanted to speak to. I gather you're about the only one who knows what's been done around this place,' with a thread of disgust evident which Ashley couldn't decide whether was meant for her, or the other members of her family.

'Well, you'll just have to wait until I return, won't you? I'm sure the others will be pleased to entertain you in the meantime,' she flouted, and determinedly headed back for the rail.

'I don't give a damn whether they will or not!' Dane ground out savagely, his fingers biting inflexibly into her soft upper arm this time and forcibly dragging her along beside him as he made for the homestead. 'So stop trying to be smart, you aggravating little brat, and get your records up to date. The last entry made in those books was over a month ago!'

Ashley tried to stop and tug herself free but was hauled unceremoniously forward again and was forced to pant her defensive, 'Well, what do you expect when there's really only two of us doing the majority of the work? There just isn't time for everything!' as they went.

'Then you'd better make time,' he suggested coldly. 'Because I want those records completed—and I want them tonight!'

'Tonight?' Ashley echoed as she stumbled up the steps and on to the verandah behind him. 'What's the rush? Why can't it wait until the weekend?'

Dane halted so suddenly that she had cannoned into him before she realised what was happening, although it didn't take her long to discover the reason for his action—it was anger!

'Because although you may not mind seeing your stock dropping like damned flies, I do!' he jeered, his eyes glittering like green ice. 'And as I happen to be in the process of buying this property as it stands, I would very much appreciate having an accurate record of the number of animals there are here so I can make arrangements to have the poor devils shipped out as soon as possible! It's a pity you didn't do the same when you received that last loan just over two years ago!' he slated her ruthlessly.

Stung into again having to defend herself, Ashley's resentment rose and she rounded on him heatedly. 'Of course I care that we're losing stock, but there hasn't been much I could do about it! I didn't use the last loan to put them out on agistment because there were so many other things which needed money spent on them, and—and I didn't think the drought would—would last as long as this,' she confessed throatily.

'Some underestimation!'

'All right, you don't have to rub it in! Don't you think I know that?' she cried anguishedly. 'But I happen to be a farmer—not a long-range weather forecaster!'

One dark brow rose satirically. 'To make out on the land you need to be something of both, although that still doesn't alter the facts. That little misjudgment on your part has effectively managed to lose you almost half your flock and your family's home!'

Briefly Ashley's eyes closed and she bit down hard on to

her bottom lip to still its trembling. 'Thanks for reminding me, it's a great comfort to know,' she tried to sound mocking, but the words only came out with a husky wretchedness, and it was fortunate Dane let her go when she spun away towards the office or she might not have been able to prevent new tears from escaping had he chosen to make any further denunciatory comments. 'I'll bring the records in when I've finished,' she murmured as she walked towards the room at the end of the verandah, but without turning her head, and without listening to hear if he even acknowledged the remark.

Immediately she had closed the office door behind her, Ashley leant back against it and surveyed the shambles before her with a despondent sigh. Something else for Dane to disparage? Determined that he shouldn't be given the opportunity to do so she hastily began clearing away the papers, periodicals, and letters which had accumulated over the months and pushed them into the bottom drawer of the steel cabinet, making a mental note to see that they were all properly filed away before he had a chance to use the office himself. That concluded, she pulled out all the relevant slips of paper she had made notes on, dockets for purchases, and anything else which required to be entered within the books her mother had replaced on the desk after taking them into town.

Once seated, though, she found it hard to concentrate on what she was supposed to be doing, for her lips could still feel the pressure of Dane's tormenting mouth against them almost as explosively as if she was still clasped in his arms, while at the same time her ears were ringing with his criticisms. The latter were a little easier to dismiss with the argument that she had always attempted to do what was best for the property, and that any misfortunes it had sustained certainly hadn't been brought about deliberately on her part. The former—that wasn't so simple to put aside— and she was at a loss to understand why she should keep remembering anyway. It had been intended only as a means to throw her off balance, and she should have been able to thrust it into the back of her mind without any hesitation

—but she couldn't—and she found herself wondering if her own impassioned response was the reason. At the mere thought of it her cheeks began to glow with mortification, and only by making herself the solemn promise that she would never again give him the means to so disarm her could she return to her work with anything like a calm mind.

For the next hour she worked on steadily, hearing in the background the muted sound of voices and occasional bursts of laughter emanating from the lounge, and her mouth pulled down at the corners with dissatisfaction. Apparently the rest of the family had been only too willing to entertain Dane!

Presently the door opened and to Ashley's surprise the object of her chagrined thoughts strode into the room bearing a steaming cup of coffee which he placed beside her. There being no other chair in the office Dane perched himself on the front corner of her desk, one long leg swinging idly. Twisting his head round in order to see what she was writing, his eyes flicked into line with hers wryly.

'You've got an impossibly sulky look about you, little one,' he taunted with a lazy smile which had her eyes diving for cover and her stomach turning somersaults. 'What's the matter? Feeling left out?'

'No, of course not!' she denied rapidly, too rapidly for him not to guess the truth, and rushed into thanking him for the coffee before adding an uneasy, 'You don't have to stay,' when he showed no signs of leaving.

Dane gave a casual shrug. 'You were taking so long I thought you might need some help.'

'No, thanks!' she refused his offer tartly. 'I shouldn't be much longer,' hoping he would take the hint and go.

But Dane showed no such inclination and continued sitting where he was, his eyes slowly surveying the small room. 'Well, at least this area looks efficient,' he commented, and Ashley's gaze flickered up to his and away again as she felt the stain of embarrassment creeping under her skin, and which wasn't helped in any way by his softly amused, 'In which drawer did you dispose of it all, Ashley?'

About to move her head in repudiation, she realised prevarication was useless and pressed her lips together in vexation, pointing silently with her pen to the appropriate drawer of the cabinet, and watching covertly out of the corner of her eye as Dane rose fluidly to his feet and sauntered around the desk. On his way back, armed with the pile of papers she had so recently thrust aside, he intercepted her glance and nodded his head obliquely towards the books in front of her.

'Better keep your mind on what *you're* doing, honey, otherwise we might be here until midnight,' he grinned annoyingly, and resumed his seat on the front of the desk.

Ashley fumed under her breath but said nothing, anxious only to get the records completed and so escape from his unwanted company, but the faster she tried to finish the work the more mistakes she made, though it wasn't until she chanced to look up and found Dane's eyes considering her intently that she became aware she had been allowing her frustrations to show, and she glared back at him aggressively.

'Did you want something? Or have I suddenly grown another couple of heads?' she quizzed sarcastically.

'No, to both questions,' he shook his head imperceptibly, but managed to give Ashley the idea that a warning had been conveyed all the same. 'I've just realised what it is that's different about you. You're wearing your hair a lot shorter these days.'

'And you don't like it?' she hazarded a mocking guess.

'On the contrary, I do like it,' came the surprisingly candid response. 'It suits you.'

Well, that settled that! If Dane Carmichael liked short hair she wouldn't be having hers cut again until it reached her ankles, Ashley decided mutinously, and after a polite, but brief, 'Thank you,' she returned to her books with a newly acquired twinkle of perverseness in the depths of her cornflower blue eyes.

However, she was soon up against the same problem she had experienced before—that of being too conscious of Dane's presence and being unable to pay all her attention to the figures she was attempting to balance because of it. The fact that she couldn't resist glancing up through her lashes in order to make out what he was reading every time the rustle of paper told her he had turned a page wasn't exactly aiding her concentration either. In the end she dropped her pen down beside the open book, leant back in her chair and folded her arms irritably.

'Well, according to my calculations, it would appear as though I've mislaid somewhere around four hundred sheep,' she informed him sardonically.

Dane's eyes didn't even rise from the letter he was perusing. 'Then you'd better re-check your figures and find them again, hadn't you, Bo-Peep?' he recommended with a decidedly cutting accent. 'I want to know exactly how many there are, and which paddocks they're in ... tonight!'

'So you said before!' she snapped just as coldly. 'And I *have* re-checked the figures—and re-checked them, and re-checked them—until my head's full of numbers chasing themselves round in circles, but I still can't account for three hundred and ninety-seven of them!'

With a smothered epithet, Dane thumped the sheath of papers he had been holding on to the desk and picked up the last book she had been working on, his eyes running knowledgeably down the marked columns, totalling as he went.

'For crying out loud, what sort of records have you been keeping?' he demanded incredulously, one finger stabbing at two separate numbers. 'Try adding those sets of figures —if it's not too much of a strain, that is—and see what total you get! How did you expect them to balance? You've entered the same amounts under two opposing headings!'

Oh, hell! Ashley nodded her comprehension and licked at dry lips, her cheeks scarlet. 'That's right, I remember now, I meant to cross out those first two entries. I—I put them in the wrong column,' she grimaced ruefully.

'Well, I hope it's not something you have a habit of doing. I've always preferred to keep a factual set of books myself.'

'And so do I, so there's no call for you to be sarcastic! I made a mistake, that's all. Or are you so infallible that it's unheard-of for you to make an error?' she widened her eyes facetiously.

'No, it's not unknown,' he admitted evenly, ignoring the impudent look. 'But I've certainly never lost almost four hundred head of stock within the pages of an account book and then claimed to have re-checked my entries.'

'I did re-check them,' she reiterated resentfully. 'But what else do you expect to happen when I know very well you're just sitting there waiting to pounce at the first opportunity if I even look like doing the smallest thing wrong?'

Dane held her belligerently reproachful gaze steadily, a corner of his mouth crooking upwards slightly. 'Are you saying I make you nervous?' he goaded dryly.

'I'm not used to working with someone breathing down my neck.'

'That didn't answer my question,' she was informed blandly, and gave him a look of pure dislike for his persistence.

'All right! Yes, you put me on edge! You always act so damned arrogantly superior!'

'Because I refuse to be stood over by some spoiled little brat?' with raised and disbelieving brows.

In her younger days that might have been true, but Ashley was in no mood to admit it. 'No! Because you just like to throw your weight around,' she jeered. 'Even when you only worked here, you couldn't resist finding fault with every solitary thing I did!'

'Someone sure needed to. You were such a . . .'

'If you call me a spoilt brat again,' she interjected furiously, 'I'll—I'll . . .' but while she was searching for an appropriate threat she gave Dane the chance to taunt mockingly,

'You'll what? Make me sorry?'

The undisguised amusement in his voice was more than Ashley could stand and she leant forward in her chair rapidly to gibe, 'You very well could be if you suddenly found yourself with the contents of that coffee cup draining over you!'

Dane rested one hand on the desk and leant towards her leisurely, although there was no matching casualness in the cool assessment of his gaze. 'I doubt it, honey, because if you're ever tempted into something so unwise, it's much more likely that you'll be the one feeling sorry for yourself afterwards,' he stated unequivocally, and then gave a cynical shrug. 'However, I wouldn't expect you to willingly take my word for it, so ... why don't you try it and we'll see?'

As much as Ashley would have loved to accept that sardonic invitation, she wasn't too sure it was the most prudent action for her to undertake, and after eyeing him heatedly for some seconds she reluctantly subsided back into her chair, but continued to hold her head challengingly high.

'Of course that's just the sort of reply I should have expected from you,' she exclaimed disdainfully. 'I bet you've never allowed a female to get the better of you, have you, Dane?'

'Not yet, honey,' he concurred lazily, his shapely mouth widening into a heart-stirring smile which set Ashley's intractable senses aglow. 'So far, I've always found it advisable to keep the upper hand—if only for my own peace of mind.'

Huh! She pulled a disgruntled face and slammed the accounts books closed. His self-assured announcement didn't come as anything of a surprise. Dane Carmichael had never given any indication of being the type who came off second best—to either male or female! But with luck perhaps he would find he had met his match in Della Marchant, she mused enjoyably, because Della never liked to be bested either! Not that Ashley had ever particularly liked their haughty neighbour, but this time she had a definite reason for hoping the older girl would succeed where others had failed.

Now she hunched her shoulders disinterestedly and suggested, 'Well, if the accounts and records were all you wanted me for ...' as she rose to her feet, preparing to leave.

'They weren't,' Dane advised promptly. 'There's a few other matters I'd like to get sorted out with you—concerning Kindyerra, of course,' he added chaffingly when her expression became suspicious. 'I would also like to have your opinion regarding some alterations I have in mind for the homestead and which I want begun as soon as possible.'

Ashley's initial astonishment quickly became submerged in angry expostulation. 'It's a little early to be talking about alterations, isn't it, Dane? Don't you think it would be better if you at least waited until you actually owned the place?'

'For God's sake, Ashley, stop taking everything as a personal affront!' he ordered exasperatedly. 'I spoke to your mother about the matter this afternoon and she was perfectly willing to give her consent to any renovations or additions I want to make taking place before the sale is finalised. Just for once, why can't you be as co-operative?'

Why couldn't she be co-operative? Considering who was talking, that was quite a joke, only Ashley didn't find it amusing. 'If you wanted co-operation, Dane, maybe you should have bought the Marchants' property instead of ours!' she tossed back pertly. 'But don't expect it from me! I didn't *ask* to stay on here, remember, *you* made it compulsory!'

Dane raked a hand through his curling dark hair and the tension growing between them in the small room was almost tangible. 'Okay, if you can't manage co-operation, at least try toleration!' he bit out sarcastically. 'But I've got more to do with my time than waste it in futile backbiting with you, so sit yourself down again and take some notes!'

A pungent reprisal rose to Ashley's lips in retaliation for being so summarily deprecated, but after one wary glance from beneath the covering of dusky lashes at his implacable expression she swallowed it grudgingly, and flounced sulkily back into her seat with a mutinous, 'I don't do shorthand,' as she picked up her pen.

'Then do it in longhand,' she was commanded peremptorily. 'But someone has to decide which paddocks need to be mustered first, and which ones last, if all those sheep out there are to be ready for transporting this weekend,' with an arm indicating angrily to the window. 'Or did you suppose they were all going to come in order when whistled?' he goaded hatefully.

'Oh, stop being so sarcastic, and stop talking as if I couldn't care less about the stock too!' she let fly with a couple of orders herself. 'The wethers in Far East will have to be moved first—they have the furthest distance to travel and Ted reckons the well out there won't last for much longer. The ewes in Near East can probably be left to last—they have the new bore we sank about six years ago and they're in the best condition.'

Dane listened to her information thoughtfully and then nodded his head in a businesslike manner. 'Right, we'll start moving the wethers into the holding and spelling paddocks to begin with. How much feed have you left in the sheds?'

'Only a little. Certainly not enough to feed that many.'

'Not even for two days?'

Sensing another indirect rebuke, Ashley replied with a vehement, 'If we could have afforded an unlimited supply of feed, our need to sell wouldn't have been so urgent, would it?' which Dane appeared to completely ignore as he went on enquiringly,

'How's the fodder situation in town, then? Is there a ready supply?'

'Sometimes,' Ashley shrugged. 'It all depends when the last shipment arrived. The whole area has been hit pretty hard and, of course, everyone's after feed because no one's been able to grow any of their own. The last consignment they brought in came from somewhere across in South Australia.'

'Okay, make a note for me to look into that in the morning,' he instructed briefly. 'Now, about the rest of them . . .'

Within half an hour Ashley had a list of notes which covered two sheets of paper itemising those matters that Dane wanted attended to during the following days and her interest, if not her admiration, had been aroused to such an extent by the speed and conciseness with which he worked that her earlier animosity had been all but forgotten, so engrossed had she become in the operation.

When at last it was all finished she looked up and put forth a tentative, 'Where are you sending them on agistment? You said something about getting in touch with Brent in here,' the tips of her fingers idly straightening the notepaper in front of her. 'Is he arranging it for you?'

Dane eased himself upright and moved across the room to study a coloured aerial photograph of the homestead and outbuildings which had been taken many years before— while his parents had owned Kindyerra, in fact—and which still hung on the wall beside the desk.

'You might say that.' He turned his head suddenly to smile down at her. 'It's Brent's station in central Queensland they'll be going to. Unlike you, they've just had one of their best seasons ever, so they should be in prime condition when they return once the drought breaks.'

'*If* it breaks,' Ashley amended automatically, her thoughts elsewhere. So Brent had his own property too. The Carmichaels must have prospered! 'And Hal and Leigh ... are they graziers as well?' she had to ask to satisfy her own curiosity.

'Uh-huh!' Dane continued with his inspection of some of the other photos on the walls.

'With big properties?' she probed a little further.

'Big enough,' came the uninformative reply as he moved on to the trophies arranged on top of the bookcase which she had won as a member of the local Pony Club.

Ashley propped her elbows on the desk and leant her chin on her linked fingers meditatively. As Dane was the eldest, wasn't it reasonable to have expected him to buy a property before his brothers, instead of after them? Unless, of course, there had only ever been one property he was interested in buying!

'But you decided to bide your time until Kindyerra came on to the market before purchasing one for yourself?'

All at once she discovered she had gained Dane's undivided attention as he turned to face her squarely, long fingers resting lightly on lean hips. 'Not exactly,' he rejected her assumption laconically, a wry smile hovering at the edges of his firm lips.

The smile as much as his uncommunicative reply sent Ashley's temper soaring. And just what was she supposed to make of that last remark? That he hadn't been waiting for Kindyerra, or that he already had a property somewhere else? Or maybe it was just his way of letting her know he didn't appreciate her enquiries into their personal affairs! If that was the case ... She rose hurriedly to her feet and rubbed the palms of her hands restively down the sides of her jeans.

'I'm sorry, it's none of my business,' she murmured huskily, refusing to meet his green and penetrating gaze. 'And—and if there's nothing else you want to know, I'll be going now,' as she moved out from behind the desk, wishing he wasn't between her and the door.

But he was, and he made no attempt to remove himself from her path. 'What's up, Ashley?' An outstretched hand barred her passage when she would have sidestepped past him, and then carried on to tilt her taut face up to his. 'For a while there I thought we might actually be going to communicate.'

Intolerably conscious of his nearness, Ashley dragged peevishly away from his touch. 'You mean, I nearly communicated with myself, don't you? Your replies were so brief I couldn't even be sure you were taking part,' she gibed.

'Honey, the only reason I didn't elaborate was because I had no wish to be accused of boasting, which knowing you, would no doubt have been the next insult to be thrown at me if I had,' the wry smile came back in force. 'You see, Kindyerra is only one of a number of properties I've bought —we have almost a dozen between the four of us,' he imparted the knowledge softly.

'Oh!' she whispered weakly, and then as the whole import of his words registered, 'Oh! I get it! You were being big-hearted enough to feel sorry for me,' she accused fiercely. 'Well, don't bother, Dane Carmichael, because I neither need nor want your pity! I can manage quite well without any sympathy from you!'

This time Ashley was past him and through the doorway before his furious *'Ashley!* Come back here!' reached out to her, but with only a defiant lift of her head to show that she had heard him, she continued on her way along the verandah without a backward look.

CHAPTER FIVE

IT seemed strange with no stock to worry over any more, reflected Ashley pensively a week and a half later as she reluctantly dressed for the party which the Marchants—or more particularly, Della—was giving on behalf of Dane and his brothers.

The days leading up to last weekend had been hectic ones, and even an objecting Janelle had been roped in to help with the rest of them when they had returned to the property after work each day. Of course she had become reconciled to the fact quite rapidly once she found she would be working alongside Leigh—the youngest of the Carmichaels—Ashley remembered with a grin, and even now was preparing for this evening's party with an enthusiasm Ashley had never seen her display before.

As for Ashley herself, she had intended to miss the party altogether, but her mother had been adamant that she attend, and rather than cause her parent any distress she had finally consented. It had also been due to Ruth's insistence that she had bought the new dress she now turned to examine critically in the mirror above her dressing table. Of swirling two-tone apricot chiffon with tiny shoestring straps which showed to advantage a wide expanse of honey-gold skin and a daringly low neckline, it clung to her curving shape provocatively, but Ashley really only saw it with half an eye, for her thoughts would keep wandering stubbornly to other issues.

To the fact that Dane now seemed to have taken sole charge of Kindyerra—with Ruth's willing permission—and with Ashley being relegated to a very minor position in the hierarchy. This had partly been brought about because until yesterday both her mother and herself had still been working out their terms of notice at Tony's restaurant in Willow Bend, but even the knowledge of the reasoning behind the circumstance couldn't make it any easier to accept in Ashley's case. The mere thought of being in a subsidiary position to Dane rankled insupportably!

There was also his attitude towards her to contend with now too. Ever since that night she had stormed out of the office so indignantly, Dane had made it painfully clear he would be taking her at her word. She had declared she didn't want either his pity or his sympathy and he was making certain he didn't give her any! So far he had faulted just about every decision she had ever made concerning the property—some for the sheer hell of it, she was positive—and for the remainder of the time ignored her completely, or deliberately set out to antagonise her, with a success rate which made Ashley shudder infuriatedly at the memory. Again and again she had vowed she would totally disregard his next goading remark, but whenever the time came for her to put her assumed indifference into practice she found it impossible to do and promptly fired back with every ounce of insolence she could manage.

Abruptly the door to her room flew open to reveal an excited Janelle standing on the threshhold, dressed in ruby red Swiss voile, the artful curls framing her glowing face indicating her increasing proficiency in her chosen career.

'Do hurry up, Ashley,' she urged plaintively. 'Lori and Alec have been here for almost ten minutes now, and we're going to be late if we don't get going soon.'

Ashley continued to smooth a silver blue shadow across her eyelids with long steady strokes. 'I fail to see how we can be since it probably won't finish until the early hours of tomorrow morning,' and she grimaced at the thought.

Janelle took in her sister's dissatisfied expression thoughtfully. 'Don't you really want to go?'

'Give the girl top marks, she just hit a bull's-eye!' Ashley retorted with a wry grin via the mirror.

'Because Dane . . . and Della will be there?'

'Hmm, Dane *and* Della. Now there's a depressing combination,' she pondered aloud, and immediately ran the two names together rapidly as, 'Dane-'n'-Della. It sounds like some exotic cattle disease,' she chuckled, blue eyes sparkling.

'Oh dear, I do wish you hadn't said it, though,' Janelle laughed. 'I'm sure I shall never be able to see them together from now on without thinking of that. I must tell . . .'

'Don't you dare!' Ashley almost dropped the lipstick she was using in her anxiety to convey her disapprobation. 'Good grief, wouldn't I be in the gun if that ever got back to a certain quarter! Believe me, he appears to have an abundant supply of ammunition to use against me now without you generously adding to it.'

'You mean Dane?' And after her sister's emphatically rueful nod, 'Oh, I wouldn't have thought he . . .'

'Well, he would! So don't mention it . . . please, Jan?'

'Okay,' the younger girl shrugged obligingly. 'But I think you're mad not to make a play for him yourself. I'm sure Lori would if she wasn't already married.'

'And you shouldn't believe all that Lori tells you. Half the time she only says things like that because she *is* safely married,' she was told in the dryest tone possible.

'You're not, though,' Janelle pointed out slyly, her dark brown eyes alight with glee. 'And you did purposely forget to reveal your thoughts regarding my suggestion, didn't you?'

Ashley clasped a delicate golden locket on a long fine chain about her neck and retaliated mockingly. 'Only because I didn't wish to shock your maidenly ears with my language. I have more consideration for my pride and self-respect than to go chasing after any man, and especially one like Dane Carmichael! He's nothing but a domineering, disparaging, sarcastic . . .'

'In other words,' Janelle broke in with a laugh, 'you don't like him any better than you ever did.'

'Understatement! I now like him less than I did before.'

Janelle decided a change of subject might be appropriate. 'What about Hal, then?' she asked, and received a long sideways look in return.

'If you're conducting some sort of matchmaking quiz on

the Carmichael males, you're way off beam, little sister.'
Ashley paused and a slow teasing grin tugged at her lips. 'I
reckon one Beaumont heart going pitter-pat whenever a
certain one of them puts in an appearance is enough—
wouldn't you agree?'

Janelle's expression turned wry. 'And here was I thinking how cleverly I was hiding it,' she laughed a little self-
consciously, and then with her eyes widening in dismay,
'You don't think Leigh's guessed, do you, Ash?'

As her sister's infatuation had stood out like a sore
thumb in Ashley's eyes, she couldn't in all honesty give
Janelle the reassurance she was obviously waiting for so
settled for what, in her mind, was the next best thing.

'If he has, he certainly doesn't seem to be averse to the
idea,' she smiled encouragingly. 'He hasn't exactly been
avoiding you, has he? I mean, just what was he doing over
here this afternoon?'

'I—um . . .' Janelle frowned in concentration. 'Actually,
I don't remember him ever getting around to telling me,'
she eventually relayed in surprise.

Ashley held both hands wide meaningfully. 'As I said . . .'
she laughed, and laying an arm around her sister's shoulders
they left the room together. Janelle anxious to be on her
way, and Ashley assuming a pseudo-smile of anticipation
for her mother's benefit.

Billambang homestead was a mass of lights and swarm-
ing with guests by the time the Beaumonts arrived, and as
she stepped from the car Ashley couldn't help but compare
the well kept grounds and buildings with the neglected
ones at Kindyerra. Everywhere the paintwork was new, the
flowering shrubs all neatly trimmed, the lawns closely
mown, and not a weed in sight.

Ramsay Marchant—Della's father—came out on to the
verandah to greet them immediately he heard the slam of
the car doors. A tall, lean, and distinguished-looking man
in his late fifties, he always had a kind word for everyone—
totally at variance with his supercilious daughter—and
now after offering greetings to them all, he caught hold of

Mrs Beaumont's hand in one of his and patted it comfortingly with the other.

'It's good to see you again, Ruth, and especially looking so well,' he complimented sincerely. 'Although I was sorry to hear that you're having to let the property go at last. That must have been a very hard decision for you to make.'

'It was, Ramsay—for all of us,' she sighed heavily. 'But we still have the future to look forward to, and Dane has been good enough to make it possible for us to stay on for another six months so that we have plenty of time to make suitable arrangements without having to rush into anything,' she deliberately lightened her tone and smiled.

'Ah, yes,' Ramsay nodded understandingly. 'I believe he has quite a few ideas for renovating the place too,' as he led the way into the house.

Ashley didn't bother to listen to her mother's reply to that statement. If it was going to develop into an admiration-for-Dane-Carmichael conversation, she wasn't interested in hearing it! Besides, she would be bound to insert a caustic denunciation somewhere in the proceedings and she knew her mother would not only be embarrassed, but extremely disappointed, if she did so when she was there as Ramsay Marchant's guest.

Their passage was a slow one to the spacious blue and cream lounge where dancing was already in progress, due to the fact that they were acquainted with just about everyone present and there were numerous greetings to be exchanged and, of course, comments regarding the impending sale to be replied to, or discussed at length in the case of particularly close friends.

When they finally did make it, Ashley noted that the room had been greatly enlarged by the glass doors which made up the outside wall having been folded back so that the wide tiled verandah could be utilised as well, and a rousing dance was taking place so that Alec almost had to shout to make himself heard over the general commotion.

'Who's for a drink?' he called after Ramsay had taken Ruth with him to speak with more friends, and Bruce had been claimed for a tête-à-tête by his girl-friend, Sheila Garrett, who had come with her parents owing to his being unable to drive over to her home and collect her.

An enquiring look at both her sisters and Lori grinned, 'I think we all are,' as of one accord they began heading towards the bar at the far end of the room.

Before they had taken many steps, however, Leigh had made his tortuous way through the crowd and a few moments later Janelle was happily forgoing any refreshments in order to join the dancers with him.

'So that's the way the wind's blowing, is it?' winked Lori. 'Now there's a young man who knew what he wanted and wasn't going to let anything stand in his way.'

Wasn't that the same for all the Carmichaels? Ashley asked herself wryly, but aloud her thoughts followed a different trend.

'Mmm, I just hope he's as serious about it as Jan appears to be,' watching with speculative eyes as her sister and her partner disappeared among the crowd. 'I wouldn't like to see her hurt, and you could hardly say the family had a good track record with regard to settling down, could you?'

'Brent's married.'

Ashley nodded in affirmation. 'So I believe. But as Mum said the other night, he always was the quiet one. He was never quite so—so . . .'

'Intensely masculine and incredibly fascinating?' put in Lori with a laugh when it looked as if Ashley was having trouble finding the right words.

A reluctantly grudging smile etched itself across slightly pensive features. 'Yes, I suppose that's what I do mean,' she was forced to admit, although it went against the grain to do so where Dane was concerned. 'Not that Brent missed out in the good looks department, but he just didn't seem to attract the female following the others did.'

'And talking about a following,' Lori murmured in an aside as she accepted a tall decorated Pimms from her husband who had reached the bar before them, 'look who's coming this way.'

Occupied with receiving her own glass from Alec, Ashley

could only spare a brief glance in the direction Lori was indicating with an expressive movement of her head, but it was sufficient to have her pulling a rueful face and awaiting Dane and Della's arrival with a tautness which was becoming frustratingly habitual the moment she knew Dane was close at hand.

Ashley took a quick sip of her drink and watched their approach uneasily. The tall redhead in purple printed organza, and the even taller dark-haired man beside her wearing a cream silk knit shirt and deep brown pants, made a striking couple, and Ashley sensed, with a strange kind of discouragement, that hers weren't the only female eyes to follow their progress attentively. Nevertheless, a heavy arm dropping casually across her shoulders had her abruptly losing concentration as she swung her head sharply to discover Hal's dark blue eyes gleaming down at her appreciatively.

'Hi, blondie,' he greeted her with an easy camaraderie. 'You look extremely ravishing tonight, if a mere male be allowed to say so. Who's the lucky feller?'

'You, naturally ... idiot!' she laughed back at him vivaciously, welcoming his uncomplicated presence in her time of need, and the imperceptible relaxing of strained nerves which accompanied it. 'Have you been dancing?' as she noticed the faint beginnings of perspiration around his hairline.

'After a fashion,' his eyes rose ceilingwards in remorseful remembrance. 'Only trouble was, she had two left feet, and with those high heels she was wearing ...' his voice trailed off significantly, and then he grimaced, 'I swear I won't be able to walk by morning!'

There was no chance for Ashley to do anything other than acknowledge his assertion with a half amused, half commiserating laugh, before the pair she had been watching previously joined them and after a bare nod of recognition to Lori and Alec, Della exclaimed in faked astonishment,

'Good heavens, it's Ashley! I didn't recognise you without the grubby jeans and dusty boots,' she smiled artlessly.

As her normal mode of apparel was dictated by the work she did about the property and not through any lack of femininity—as Della was very well aware—Ashley only shrugged indifferently in response to the malicious remark and left it to an apparently willing Hal to come to her defence.

'How could you possibly mistake her?' he asked, his brows rising incredulously. 'No one else round here has that beautiful wheat-gold hair,' with his fingers gently ruffling through its silken texture admiringly.

Though somewhat taken aback by Hal's championship of her neighbour, Della didn't let the unexpectedness of it faze her for long.

'But you forget, Hal, that these days I normally only see Ashley from a distance when I'm taking my morning ride, and on those occasions her head's always covered by a scruffy-looking hat and she's just a dim outline in the middle of a cloud of dust,' she declared reproachfully, lips pouting. 'For all I knew, Ashley could have dyed her hair.'

'People usually change their hair to my colour, Della . . . not the other way around.' Ashley spoke up for herself this time, mockingly.

From her potentially supported position beside Dane, her arm linked proprietorially with his, Della smiled patronisingly. 'I know,' she purred spitefully. 'But I thought that, in your case, seeing your hair must have a continual reddish tinge from all that dust on Kindyerra, you might have decided to change it to my colour permanently,' she laughed and put a careful hand to her own fashionably arranged auburn curls.

'Then maybe you're the one who ought to be changing,' Hal chipped in with a broad grin. 'Otherwise people might think all that flaming colour of yours is nothing more than an accumulation of that dust you keep mentioning.'

Although Della's brown eyes narrowed threateningly and she was obviously on the brink of some devastating retort, it was Dane who made the cutting comment,

'Which really isn't a laughing matter, Hal, considering it's possible to watch that damn topsoil disappearing whenever the slightest wind springs up. The place should have been cleared of stock months ago!' The direction of his gaze clearly showed for whom his grim reprimand had been meant.

'That's just what I've always said!' Della couldn't wait to add her denigrating contribution. 'It's just been allowed to deteriorate into nothing more than a dustbowl!'

If she says that word once more . . .! Ashley gritted her teeth furiously, but her spoken resentment was all reserved for the man next to the gloating redhead.

'Then why bother buying the place?' she demanded caustically. 'If it's in such a poor condition as you're insinuating, I wouldn't have thought it was worth your while.'

'It would have been even less profitable to have left it in your hands and have all that mortgage money tied up for God only knows how long!' Dane ground out so contemptuously that Ashley took an involuntary step backwards. 'Besides, I happen to care for the property and it seemed a good time to step in, while there was still something left to salvage!'

In the momentary frozen silence which followed Dane's savage condemnation, Ashley caught her bottom lip between her teeth so hard she wondered she didn't bite right through it, every particle of colour draining from her face as agonised blue eyes clung to his disbelievingly, and then everyone regained their voices simultaneously.

Lori's gasped, 'That's unfair, Dane!' being supplanted by her husband's censuring, 'Hey, steady on, old son!' which held sway until Della's approving, 'It's about time somebody looked after it,' was overtaken by Hal's gruffly protective, 'Come on, blondie! I don't know about you, but I've heard enough for one evening!' as his arm tightened about Ashley's shaking figure and, after relieving her of her drink and placing it on the bar, he steered her unresistingly among the gyrating dancers.

But it was impossible for Ashley to match her steps to the music—she couldn't even hear the music, in fact, in her shocked state—and she shook her head weakly.

'I'm sorry, Hal,' she whispered apologetically. 'But would

you mind if—if we went outside? I think I'm going to cry.' She tried to make a joke of it but had to clamp down on her trembling lip again to prevent the foreboding from becoming a humiliating fact.

Without another word Hal guided her out on to the verandah with a supporting arm about her slender waist, only speaking when he pushed open the screen door so she could precede him into the gardens.

'Hell! What can I say, Ashley?' he sighed with one last doubtful look over his shoulder to where Dane was still standing near the bar, their eyes meeting and holding challengingly, before he followed her down the steps. 'I know you and Dane have always struck sparks off each other but, God, I've never known him to slate a member of the opposite sex like that in my life!'

Ashley swallowed hard and moved her head helplessly. 'It's just that he seems so determined to imply that everything I've done is wrong! Some—some of my decisions were, I know, but not all of them, Hal, not all of them!' she cried despairingly, the tears she had managed to suppress now refusing to be denied any longer and spilling on to her thick lashes.

Hal groaned and pulled her comfortingly close against his chest, one hand stroking soothingly up and down the back of her neck. 'I know, blondie, I know,' he murmured. 'I can't fathom him out right at the moment either.'

The snap of the screen door swinging closed had him looking up swiftly, although Ashley made no attempt to do the same, but on feeling his arms tightening even more securely about her and the tense stillness about him which ensued, she at last raised her own head to follow the direction of his unwavering gaze.

'Take a walk, Hal! Ashley and I have unfinished business to settle,' Dane advised inflexibly, thumbs hooking into the back of the wide leather belt which encircled his lithe waist.

'Take one yourself, Dane! I doubt that Ashley wants to hear anything else you might have to say!' Hal returned just as adamantly and making no move whatsoever to do as had been suggested.

A muscle stirred ominously beside Dane's outthrust jaw and his eyes raked thunderously over his brother. 'And when I want your opinion I'll ask for it!' he rasped. 'Now . . . bow out, Hal, before this gets out of hand!'

'I'm damned if I will!' came the growled retort. 'So do your worst and we'll see just who it is that bows out, won't we?' setting Ashley gently to one side.

'Oh, no, Hal!' Ashley caught at his left arm imploringly when it became evident neither of them had the slightest intention of giving way to the other.

Indeed it had come as something of a surprise that the normally easy-going Hal would make such a defiant stand on her behalf, but on seeing the two of them facing each other so implacably had brought the realisation that underneath his even-tempered exterior he possessed the same unyielding tenacity his brother did, and that made the situation even more precarious than she had originally believed.

'Not on my account, please!' she continued tearfully when the tension between them showed no signs of slackening. 'I'll—I'll talk to him. Who knows? Maybe he's come to apologise,' she proposed bitterly, and completely unbelieving of the words she uttered.

At last some of the rigidity left Hal's stance—almost as if he saw the unlikely possibility of her doubting suggestion taking place—and for the first time since Dane had followed them outside, Hal's glance dropped from his brother's and focused intently on Ashley.

'You don't have to if you don't want to,' he assured her grimly.

'I know—thank you, Hal,' she smiled tremulously, her fingers still clutching his arm as though frightened that if she released it he would immediately adopt his previously threatening pose. 'And I can—can always call you if I need you,' she unconsciously offered a warning of her own to Dane.

Hal's fingers curved over hers and squeezed reassuringly. 'As long as you remember that,' he acceded meaningfully with a rallying smile. And as he passed his brother on his way back to the house, 'You keep it in mind too, Dane!' much more pointedly. 'We may not disagree often but, by heaven, I won't be standing by and letting you rip into Ashley again for some inexplicable reason only you yourself know about!'

Dane's reply was conveyed by the flexing of wide shoulders and the lightly mocking lift to one dark brow, but with Hal's departure Ashley suddenly became mistrustful of her legs' ability to keep her upright and she rapidly made for a rustic plank seat which had been built around the vase of a large pink-berried pepper tree.

'Very touching! I had no idea Hal was so chivalrous,' Dane drawled sardonically as he stood looking down on her drooping head. 'But don't hold your breath waiting for that apology, honey, because you're out of luck!' His tone reverting to one of cold anger as he abruptly leant one hand against the tree to take his weight and the other gripped her chin roughly to force her tear-stained face up to his. 'And don't you dare gaze so accusingly up at me again with those great big tortured eyes of yours like you did inside!' he commanded furiously. 'You were the one who said you didn't want or need any pity or sympathy, so don't criticise me when the going gets rough! If you're finding it too much of a strain, perhaps you should consider retracting the statement!' as he released his hold on her dismissively and pushed himself away from the tree to stand with his arms folded menacingly across his chest.

'And wouldn't you just love that!' the sarcastic words tumbled from Ashley's lips almost of their own volition, and her eyes began to blaze a vivid blue. 'To have me admitting that you've won, and to come crawling on my hands and knees begging for quarter! Well, nothing doing!' She leapt to her feet to give vent to her feelings. 'I'd rather die than be reduced to asking for mercy from you!' she flung at him melodramatically, her breasts heaving, her hands forming nerveless fists at her sides.

His green eyes suddenly crinkled at the corners, Ashley couldn't be certain whether through anger or amusement. 'Brave words, honey,' he gibed lazily. 'Let's hope you have the courage of your convictions . . . this time.'

'I had them before, Dane! I just hadn't realised you were intending to turn it into a no-holds-barred contest for everyone to watch,' she was stung into retorting acidly.

'And now that you know?'

The softly spoken words had her searching his face warily. There had been some shade to his tone that she couldn't quite put her finger on, but the thought of it was somehow making her uneasy and she licked nervously at dry lips.

'I—well, you won't catch me unawares next time, will you? I shall know what to expect,' she declared in a voice as confident as she could make it under the circumstances.

'You think so?' He smiled so devastatingly that Ashley was too occupied in trying to quell her reeling emotions to notice he had moved until she felt an imprisoning hand sliding to a halt within her hair and he taunted, 'Then I'll just have to keep changing my tactics, won't I?' as his mouth lowered unavoidably to take possession of hers in a kiss which caught her totally unprepared and had her lips parting invitingly beneath his before she could regain control of her turbulent senses.

Even so, she was mortifyingly aware that it was Dane who had freed her rather than she who had broken away when at last they separated, and she rushed into protective speech in an effort to not only vindicate herself but to deprecate him.

'Good try, Dane,' she applauded with a mocking lift to her chin, 'but I'm afraid you're wasting your time. You see, it failed completely to have the disconcerting effect you were hoping for. In fact, it didn't affect me at all,' she lied blatantly, hoping against hope he couldn't hear the irregular thumping of her heart which sounded betrayingly loud to her own ears, or sense the turmoil within her which she was so valiantly trying to overcome.

His eyes swept over her defiant figure slowly, tantalisingly, and Ashley flushed a bright pink. 'I would never have guessed,' he drawled lazily.

Ashley caught a soft lower lip between her teeth undecidedly. His mockery was ambiguous in the extreme, but she suspected only she would be the more discomposed if the subject was pursued further, and in consequence shied away from it swiftly.

'Yes, well, if that concludes our unfinished business for the evening, I would like to be getting back to the party— provided you have no other stratagems you wish to experiment with, of course,' she allowed finely arched brows to ascend sardonically.

'None right at the moment, honey, but I'll keep you posted,' as he swept an arm wide to indicate that she had an unobstructed passage to the homestead, and then fell into step beside her when she took advantage of the gesture.

'Mmm, do,' Ashley couldn't refrain from challenging with mock-sweetness. 'And I'll even try to remember that you like to fight dirty, so you don't find me as easily routed next time.'

'Your thoughtfulness is overwhelming.'

'And so is your arrogance!' she snapped. 'But you always were a sarcastic and aggravating beast, weren't you, Dane?'

'Only to impudent brats,' he allowed, lightly jeering.

Ashley's eyes flashed with anger at the term, but she refused to lose her temper. 'Unfortunately for you, though, I've grown some since those days. You can hardly resort to spanking and a ducking as a means of retaliation now.'

Dane spared her a long, amused look of irony. 'I wouldn't rely too heavily on that assumption, if I were you,' he recommended.

She should have known! Her gaze slid down the lean muscular length of him and back to his face derisively. 'Ah, yes, there's always brute force when all else fails, isn't there?' she conceded disparagingly. 'Although I might remind you that I wasn't an easy victim last time, and I'll be even less so if you're ever rash enough to try anything of that sort again. I managed to give you quite a few scratches to remember me by,' she recalled pleasurably.

'A scar from one of which I still carry,' Dane relayed ruefully, an expressive hand rubbing at the side of his neck.

'Oh!'

Somehow she found that disclosure not quite so pleasant. Of course her relationship with Dane had always been an intense one, but even so the thought that she had actually marked someone's skin for life was a little distasteful.

'Well, I—I'm sorry about that,' she apologised, albeit a trifle grudgingly. 'But what about *my* feet?' as she chanced upon a recollection which served to alleviate her discomfort while returning her to an attacking position.

'Your feet?' Dane's eyes mirrored his puzzlement.

'Yes, my feet!' was repeated resentfully. 'When you drove off in such a flaming temper that day you took my sandals in the back of the ute with you,' she complained. 'And the ground was too hot to walk on, so I had to hop from clump to clump all the way home like some incapacitated kangaroo!' On seeing the beginnings of a smile quirking the corners of his mouth she broke off to order belligerently, 'And don't you dare laugh! It wasn't funny—there were burrs everywhere—catheads mainly,' with a shudder as she recalled how deeply their three-pronged spikes had penetrated her unprotected flesh. 'My feet were in a horrible mess by the time I finally got back, and I could hardly stand—or sit—for the best part of the next week!'

'Then why didn't you wait for someone to come and collect you?'

'I probably didn't think of it,' she confessed wryly, finding her normal sense of humour refusing to be suppressed, so that in the end she had no choice but to grin candidly, 'Besides, I was in too much of a hurry to reach the homestead so I could tell everyone how beastly you'd been.'

The sound of sheer enjoyment in Dane's delightfully attractive laughter sent the blood shooting through Ashley's veins chaotically, but its rate became even more hectic when he put both hands on her shoulders, swung her around to face him, and with a laughing, 'I love you,' dropped a light kiss on the top of her forehead.

Bemused, Ashley offered no resistance whatsoever when he laid a casual arm across her shoulders and they started forward again. She was too intent on comparing her present dislocated feelings to those when, as a child, she had been herding some calves into the race and one of them had suddenly lashed out with its hind feet, catching her in the stomach and sending her sprawling. It was the same kind of sickening paralysis she was experiencing now on discovering that she didn't want to hear those particular words from Dane in amused approval for her self-mocking honesty—she wanted to hear them because he *meant* them!

There was no time to dwell further on the matter, however, for the next moment Dane pushed open the screen door and Hal paced forward quickly out of the shadows, his brows rising quizzically at the sight of his brother's arm holding her so firmly against his side.

'Safe, sound, and all in one piece.' Dane sent a mocking glance in Hal's direction as he sketched them both a brief salute and continued on into the lounge with a long-legged stride without waiting to see if they were intending to follow or not.

'Everything's back to normal, I see,' Hal's head nodded wryly after his brother.

With pensive eyes following Dane's progress across the crowded room to where Della was the centre of a small group, Ashley released her corroborating, 'Yes, everything's back to normal,' on a despondent note, but upon Hal's lightly enquiring, 'Feel more like dancing now?' she pulled herself together rapidly and gave him her answer with an almost natural smile.

'I'd love to, Hal. I think that's just what I need at the moment.'

A chance to get my mind off your tormentingly male elder brother and back into perspective, she continued to herself ruefully. It had been abundantly clear from the expression on Dane's face when he rejoined Della that he had undergone no such startling illumination as she had, and he had certainly never given her any reason to suspect that he was likely to in the future either! So the faster she stopped thinking about him in that fashion the better off she would be. It was preferable by far that he continue to think of her as a precocious brat than for him to gain an inkling as to just how radically her feelings towards him had altered!

For the remainder of the evening it was impossible for anyone to guess that Ashley wasn't enjoying herself as much as she appeared as she determinedly danced the night away. Although not once did Dane ask her to dance, she noted acidly, because it seemed he couldn't drag himself out of Della's arms long enough to spare the time for more than a few duty dances. A fact which didn't go unnoticed by the other guests either, and which was the subject of some quite considerable speculation by the time supper was served.

But once the party came to an end and they had returned home the same thoughts persistently came to disturb her immediately she turned out her bedroom light, preparing for sleep. Oh, God! She suddenly sat up again, her hands pressed to cheeks which were already staining, even in the darkness. Could he have guessed all those years ago that that was why she was always so much ruder and more insolent to him than anyone else? she groaned distraughtly, feeling her insides curl with embarrassment. But how else could a pigtailed schoolgirl hope to obtain the attention of an attractive twenty-two-year-old who could have his pick of any girl in town—even if she wasn't aware it was an unknown jealousy which was making it seem so imperative! And he could quite easily have suspected that was the cause —she threw herself prone again in despair, but with a smothered yelp when she connected with the headboard instead of her pillow. Dane was certainly no one's fool—he never had been!

A realisation which did little to relieve Ashley's current anxieties, and the next hours were spent restlessly tossing back and forth until she finally awakened to a pink and pearl dawn, feeling less than rested, and with her skin faintly damp from perspiration.

CHAPTER SIX

LATE on Sunday afternoon, Ashley was laboriously tran-
scribing the last of the scrawled notes that Dane had given
her after lunch on to the letter she had in the portable
typewriter when a lengthening shadow appeared on the
office floor and she looked towards the doorway to find her
sister hovering just outside.

'Am I interrupting?' Janelle half smiled hesitantly.

'No, I'm almost finished,' Ashley sighed and enjoyably
stretched her arms above her head. 'Come on in and take a
pew.' She waved a hand to the front of the desk and
grinned, 'We'll have to see about getting another chair in
here,' as her sister pushed herself up on to the polished
wood.

Janelle spent some time playing with the string of beads
she had strung around her neck and then smiled again
weakly. 'I had—um—something I wanted to ask you,' she
revealed at last.

'I'd already gathered that,' Ashley laughed, and then her
head inclined sideways with a slight frown to match the
one already creasing her sister's troubled forehead. 'So
what's the problem? I'm not that hard to talk to, am I?'

'Oh, no,' Janelle flashed a swift smiling protest. 'It's just
that this—er—concerns the Carmichaels.' She let out her
breath heavily and went back to fiddling with her beads.

Outwardly Ashley showed no change in her expression,
but only due to a rigid disciplining of her facial muscles.
Inwardly her nerves were constricting ungovernably. 'And
what about the Carmichaels?' she managed to ask lightly.

'Well, I know how you feel about them,' Janelle spread
her hands wide implicitly. 'Although this is really only
about Leigh.'

'So . . .?'

Her sister took a deep breath and the words came out in a rush. 'So Leigh was thinking of asking Mum if he could move in here instead of staying at Billambang. We certainly have the room, and as all three of them spend most of their days working here anyway, he thought he might as well save the time it takes in riding or driving over and—and . . .'

'Maybe get to see more of you at the same time?' quizzed Ashley with a relieved laugh. She hadn't known quite what to expect, but this was certainly nothing to get uptight about.

'I hope so,' Janelle confessed with feeling, her cheeks flushed, her brown eyes glowing.

'But I'm still not sure where I come into it. Were you after my opinion as to whether Mum would say yes or no?' Ashley hazarded, perplexed.

'Not really. I just thought it would be best if I sounded you out on the matter before Leigh mentioned it to her. As I said, I know how you feel about them.'

'And you thought I would veto the idea, is that it?' Ashley jumped forward to the edge of her seat in reproachful disbelief. 'Oh, hell, Jan, you should know better than that! I've got nothing against Leigh or Hal—I never did have. For heaven's sake, invite him here if you want to—it's not my house.' She sank wearily back into her chair, disappointment uppermost.

'I'm sorry, Ash,' Janelle put out a conciliatory hand tentatively. 'I guess I should have known, but it's just that . . .'

'I usually say "the Carmichaels" when in actual fact I'm really only referring to one of them,' Ashley finished for her ruefully. 'I'm sorry for shouting at you too, Jan, and especially when it's not your fault. Speak to Mum by all means—I've got nothing against it.'

'Do you think she'll agree?'

'I don't see why not. As you so rightly said, we have the room, and you know Mum—the more the merrier.'

'Mmm, that's the way I'm hoping she sees it.'

Ashley eyed the younger girl with some amusement.

'There is one thing you might explain for me, though,' she smiled.

'And that is?'

'How come you're so interested in someone who's obviously a dyed-in-the-wool grazier when you can't stand station life?' she said dryly.

Janelle had the grace to blush but immediately defended herself with an excusing, 'Oh, it's not really that I don't like living on a station—it's just that I don't like working out *there*,' with an outflung hand to signify the great expanse of land beyond the window. 'If I'm left alone to potter around the homestead I'm okay.'

'In that case, you'd better make sure any grazier you choose is wealthy enough to keep you there,' Ashley grinned.

'He is,' came the prompt reply, whereupon Janelle's colour deepened considerably upon receipt of an upward-slanting glance from beneath thick curling lashes.

Once her sister had departed, Ashley completed her typing quickly in order to make sure she had left the office before Dane returned, and after placing the correspondence in a pile on the desk to await his signature she slipped the cover over the old machine and stepped out on to the verandah, shielding her eyes against the glare of a descending sun.

'You see? I told you the next owner would care,' Ted called out with a broad grin as he passed the homestead in front of her, apparently on his way to the machine shed. 'Already things are starting to happen around here, eh?'

Ashley wrinkled her nose wryly and hurried down the steps so she could keep pace with him. 'So what has our great and glorious boss found fault with and ordered changed today?' she mocked.

'You can't blame him for feeling dissatisfied, Ashley,' the old man reproved gently. 'Kindyerra was never in anything but first class condition when his family lived here. You should be pleased to see all the work they're putting into it.'

'Oh, I suppose I am really,' she hunched away from his

admonishment restively. 'Or I would be if he didn't keep insisting that I've deliberately let the place become run-down!'

Ted didn't think it wise to pursue the point. 'The ideas he has in mind for the house please you, though, hmm?'

'I—er—I don't know, actually,' she had to admit, but reluctantly. If she remembered correctly, she hadn't exactly allowed him a chance to get around to the subject that first evening he had ridden over to see them, and ever since she had been too proud to ask. 'Just what has he got planned for the house?'

'Perhaps he would prefer to tell you himself.'

'I doubt it,' she grimaced, adding a silent 'not now, any-way' for her own benefit, before continuing in her most cajoling tone, 'Come on, Ted, what's he told you?'

By the time he had completed the narration they had come to a halt beside the ute parked outside the shed and Ashley was staring at him in wide-eyed amazement.

'Good grief, all that comprises major renovations!' she gasped. 'I only thought it would be a new coat of paint and maybe a touch up here and there.' A look of deep concentration settled over her forehead and she eyed him suspiciously. 'In fact, why is he going to so much trouble? Is he planning to live here himself?'

'Why wouldn't he?'

'I—well, no reason, I suppose,' she shrugged. 'Except that he obviously has a home elsewhere which he's been living in quite happily until now.'

'Perhaps he likes this one better—because it's bigger,' Ted inserted blandly as he threw the first of several rolls of wire into the back of the ute.

'And why would a bachelor need such a large house?' Ashley immediately began to scoff, only to stop open-mouthed as the full import of Ted's words sank in. 'Unless, of course . . . he isn't planning on staying a bachelor much longer,' she answered her own question flatly, soberly.

Ted removed his hat in order to wipe an arm across his forehead and then settled it back in place, his eyes watching her closely. 'The idea doesn't suit you?' he probed.

'Heavens! Why should it matter to me?' she prevaricated desperately, forcing a look of utter unconcern on to her features by willpower alone. 'I've made it no secret what I think of Dane. I hope she gives him hell!' she laughed mockingly, but had to turn away straight afterwards and pretend an interest in the loosened sheet of iron on the shed roof which a sudden gust of wind had set to banging discordantly, and so prevent him from seeing the anguish which she was sure would be all too apparent in the depths of her eyes.

Surveying the delicate profile outlined against an almost colourless sky, Ted shook his head and sighed. 'Did you want a lift out to Stony Gully to see what's been done to-day?'

That had originally been her intention, but now Ashley discarded it abruptly. 'No! No, thanks, Ted,' she amended her refusal a little more softly. 'I think I'll take Amarina out for a while. She hasn't done much work of late and she'll be getting fat and lazy if I'm not careful,' she smiled faintly, half turning back to him but not quite all the way. She still didn't trust herself to stand up under a full inspection.

With an acknowledging finger raised to the brim of his hat, Ted pulled open the driver's door and slid inside the vehicle, starting the engine and heading northwards as Ashley morosely kicked at a stone in her path and wandered in the direction of the yards.

A while later she skirted the banks of the now bone-dry dam and reined the mare to a halt beneath the same coolibah she had rested her back against that humiliating day ten years before, suddenly wishing she had chosen another route for her ride.

Dismounting, she slid the reins forward over Amarina's head and stood looking across to where Dane had been working on the corner post which served the three adjoining paddocks. She could still see the green eyes blazing with fury as he stalked across the open ground towards the creek, and still feel the choking panic which had risen within her throat as she scrambled to her feet with the realisation that, for the first time in her life, she was about to be made to take the consequences for her impertinence.

Dane couldn't be aware of it, of course, but his treatment of her that day had been a turning point in her young life, she mused as she walked a short distance along the creek bank. Never again had she ever dared to speak to anyone else in that manner and from then on she had begun to stop and consider the effect her words might have—and more importantly, what repercussions they might bring— should she be reckless enough to voice them. Until Dane had come back into her life, that was! With him she could no more have put a brake on her scathing words than she could ... swim in a dry creek!

And discovering she was in love with him hadn't made it any easier—quite the reverse, in fact! Now she had no choice but to continue with her barbed remarks for her own protection—whether she might otherwise have wanted to or not. Despondently, she retraced her steps and gathering up the reins she swung back into the saddle, urging the mare forward automatically.

She also had the thought of Dane getting married in the not too distant future to contend with now as well. A thought she had been deliberately refusing to contemplate ever since Ted had brought the suggestion out into the open. And why? Because it brought such a stabbing pain to the region of her ribs whenever it crept surreptitiously back into her mind that she felt as if she would never recover from the aching torment of it. The hurt she had experienced at losing Kindyerra was nothing compared to the sense of desolation which overwhelmed her at the idea of Dane being married—to someone else! Not that she could ever really have hoped he might, given time, come to consider her as a non-sparring partner, but perhaps even that she could have come to terms with if he at least had remained single. As it was ... She shook her head cheerlessly and heeled Amarina into a faster gait, intent on taking the longest way home.

When she finally arrived back at the homestead, though, she knew that decision to have been a mistake, because the

men had all returned from Stony Gully by then and were
clustered around the horse yard, unsaddling.

'Where on earth have you been, Ash?' Janelle suddenly
appeared from behind Leigh's bay gelding, her face worried. 'It's been two and a half hours since you told Ted you
were going for a ride.'

Had it really been that long? Ashley's eyes searched the
purpling sky for confirmation and she shrugged offhandedly.
'I didn't realise—but I've been gone for longer before this.'

'But not without anyone knowing the direction you'd
taken,' Dane's deep voice censured coolly as he moved in
between the chestnut and the black, his arms reaching up
to lift her from Amarina's back. 'We were beginning to
worry about you.'

'Oh, that's ridiculous! I know every acre of this property
like the back of my hand!' she exclaimed, kicking her feet
irritably free of the stirrups because, unless she wished to
make a scene, she had no option but to allow Dane's hands
to clasp about her slender waist and lower her to the
ground.

'But Ted also said he thought you might have been upset
over something when you left.' Dane's fingers gripped
deeper into her flesh as he swung her against his chest,
seeming determined to keep her a suspended captive until
she answered.

Ashley's immediate reaction was to damn Ted for an old
meddler. But she was so devastatingly aware of the sensuous feel of Dane's body along the whole of her length that
it was nearly impossible to guide her thoughts rationally
at all and she glowered at him stormily.

'Put me down!' she commanded through clenched teeth
so the others couldn't hear, her hands pushing against his
wide shoulders in an ineffectual effort to force him into
releasing her. 'Of—of course I wasn't upset! Why should I
be?' she countered fiercely, defensively.

For a reply Dane smiled mockingly. 'You tell me,' he invited softly.

'There's nothing to tell!' she struggled furiously. But as
this only made her all the more conscious of how closely

she was moulded against his masculine shape, she halted almost as soon as she started with a supplicating, 'So please let me go, Dane.'

His grasp didn't lessen one whit. 'Wasn't it only two nights ago that you vowed you would rather die than plead for mercy from me?' he taunted banteringly, his smile broadening as her scowl increased.

'*You* . . .!'

Ashley didn't bother to complete her denunciation, she just brought her right hand back and let it fly for the side of his face. Only his reflexes were too sharp, and he released her so quickly that as she dropped to the ground she lost all the momentum from her swing and ended with her fingers clinging about his neck in order to keep her balance.

Before she could pull away from him, Dane's hands had come up to grip hers about the wrists, spinning her around so that she had her back to him, his hands retaining their grasp as he folded his arms tightly about her midriff.

'That's a no-no!' she heard him whisper annoyingly beside her right ear. 'Next time, make sure you're not gone so long,' came the arrogant order as he took his arms away to give her an emphasising slap on the seat of her jeans and accompanied it with an urging push in the direction of her mount.

'Go to hell! I'll be gone for as long as I wish!' Ashley spun around to mutter fervently at his departing figure, but the unwavering look of warning he turned to deliver had her biting at her lip uneasily and ruefully admitting that maybe it would be wiser if she reconsidered on that last defiance after all. The look in his eyes had been far too reminiscent of other years for her liking!

'Hey! What's this I hear about Leigh moving across to Kindyerra?' Hal paused in the act of pulling the saddle from his chestnut to peer across its back questioningly at Ashley.

'Just that, I guess,' she laughed wryly. 'Although it will save him all that time wasted in travelling from Billambang to here and then back again every day.'

'Oh, yeah, it'll do that okay,' he drawled humorously as he tossed his saddle up on to the rail of the yard and half turned to catch his younger brother's eye. 'Not that I've ever known him to be quite that anxious to get on with the job before, mind you. I could have sworn a little brown-eyed brunette had something to do with it myself.'

Leigh's grey eyes glittered cheerfully in the approaching dusk. 'Shut your mouth, Hal, before you find yourself flat on your back,' he threatened with a grin amid the general laughter. 'Just because you didn't think of the idea first, there's no need to let your envy show,' he taunted.

Hal pushed his hat to the back of his head and grinned in acknowledgment. 'And the trouble with you is you have no sympathy in your soul for your fellow man,' he retorted with a suitably pained look. 'Two weeks of watching next door's redhead acting as if Dane's her exclusive property is enough for anyone.'

'Shut your mouth, Hal, before you find yourself flat on your back,' Dane's voice reached out to them in a dry repeat of Leigh's earlier prediction as he shouldered his saddle into the shed. 'Della's been extremely helpful since she invited us to stay with her and her father.'

'She may have been to you, old son,' Hal laughed after him undaunted. 'But I can't say I've noticed Leigh or myself receiving the same sort of devoted attention.' He swung back to Ashley and winked. 'Touchy pair, aren't they? Maybe you and I should get together so we're not left out in the cold.'

With her head lifting defiantly in retaliation for Dane's ironically arching brows on overhearing the suggestion when he returned to his mount, Ashley nodded to Hal agreeably. 'Sounds like a great idea,' she smiled as he prepared to take his own saddle inside the shed.

'Don't take him seriously, Ashley, he only meant it in fun,' Dane advised gravely a few seconds later after sending his stallion into the yard with a smack on its rump. 'Hal has never been one for lasting relationships.'

Something Ashley hadn't needed telling—she already knew! 'But seeing how you're four years older than he is and still single, you are, I suppose?' she gibed scornfully. 'But thanks for the overpowering compliment! It's a great morale-builder to know you don't think I have what it takes to change his mind!'

'That wasn't what I meant, and you know it!'

'Then what did you mean?' she demanded, purposely ignorant. 'That you couldn't see how Hal could possibly be interested in *me*?'

Dane's hands came to rest heavily on his hips and his head tilted skywards as if seeking heavenly aid as a stifled expletive was ground between his lips.

'No, that wasn't what I meant either, you infuriating, word-twisting little . . .'

'Come on, you two, break it up.' Hal pushed himself between them with a grin and gathered up Ashley's equipment. 'Good lord, I've never known two people for rubbing each other the wrong way as much as you do. What started it this time, anyway?' as he looked from one to the other.

'I tried to caution Ashley about not taking your suggestion seriously that the pair of you team up,' Dane was the one to reveal the cause sardonically.

'Well, there was no need to,' Hal enlightened him obligingly, and causing Ashley to suck in her breath sharply for fear of what he might disclose next. 'Ashley already knew I was only joking. We read each other pretty well, don't we, blondie?'

Ashley's eyes closed tightly with dismay and even in the half light it was plain to see the colour spreading over her soft skin as she reluctantly endorsed his belief with a practically inaudible, 'Mmm.'

'One of these days . . .!' Dane's lips clamped together relentlessly and Ashley could see just how much discipline he was having to exercise in order to hold his temper in check. 'One of these days, honey, you're going to provoke me into settling our account once and for all. Don't say you haven't been warned!'

Hal watched his brother stride for the homestead in astonishment. 'For crying out loud, what was *that* for?'

'Private war . . . no independent observers allowed,'

Ashley half laughed with an uncontrollable shiver, troubled eyes following Dane's rapid progress with misgivings until he disappeared from view.

'Ashley, love?' The unusually worried note in Hal's voice had her swinging to face him more quickly than she would otherwise have done. 'I don't profess to know what it is with the two of you, and maybe it's better I don't,' he smiled a little ruefully, one hand stretching out to ruffle her hair in brotherly fashion. 'But do yourself a favour, hmm? For God's sake, tread warily for a while till he's had a chance to cool off! I haven't seen Dane this close to completely losing his temper for years—probably not since we were here before,' he put in dryly. 'But I'm afraid for your pretty neck, little one ... you have a bad habit of laying it on the line all too readily!'

'He deliberately sets out to aggravate me too, Hal,' she felt bound to defend herself resentfully. 'It's not always my fault!'

'Sure he does, little one, but you know as well as I do that this goes back an awful long way. And which came first, huh? The chicken or the egg?'

'You're saying I should be the one to surrender?'

'Hell, I'm not sure quite what I'm suggesting. I've never tried my hand at social counselling before,' he grinned. 'Although surrendering, as you put it, hadn't really entered my mind. I was thinking more along the lines of a different attitude, perhaps.'

'Change my tactics, you mean?' she unconsciously quoted the words Dane had uttered at the Marchants' party.

He nodded in approval. 'Mmm, that's more like it.'

Leigh led his bay out into the yard and turned him loose. 'Are you coming, or are you going to stand here talking all night?' he smiled as he passed them on his way back.

'Nearly finished,' Hal acknowledged, finally heading for the shed with Ashley's gear as she urged Amarina through the gateway. 'But you go on ahead, we'll be up in a couple of minutes.'

'Okay,' Leigh agreed easily as he and Janelle also made for the homestead, leaving Ashley to query a trifle sardonically when Hal rejoined her by the rail, 'Do you also have some particular tactic in mind which you would suggest I change to?'

'Don't be difficult, love, I'm expecting you to contribute something to the scheme,' he chuckled incorrigibly. 'Doesn't that feminine intuition you females are supposed to have in abundance tell you anything? You must be able to think of something which doesn't involve head-on confrontation.'

Ashley pushed her hands into the pockets of her jeans, her manner thoughtful. 'I—I'll think about it,' was all she could promise at the moment.

She was as aware as Hale that if her reactions to Dane continued in the same way for much longer there was going to be one almighty showdown in the all too near future. But unfortunately, with her emotions as deeply involved as they were, she couldn't think of any other method which would conceal them quite so thoroughly.

A short time later, as she stood beneath the warm fall of the shower, Ashley found herself wishing that her mother had chosen some other evening to invite the Carmichaels to stay for dinner. It wasn't that she minded Hal and Leigh's presence, of course, but she was extremely apprehensive of her next meeting with Dane and would far rather have had it occur a few days hence. A few days during which she might have had the opportunity to arrange her thoughts more neatly regarding this afternoon's revelations.

Initially it had been Ted's inference regarding an impending marriage for Dane which had set her emotions on their downward spiralling path, but when this had been coupled with the information that Della was behaving as though Dane was the number one contender on her short list, then Ashley's thoughts became even more despairing than she would ever have believed possible. It was too painful to even contemplate for one moment the mental picture of Della Marchant lording it over the homestead and property she had always loved so dearly.

In fact, she was so unenthusiastic about the evening ahead that after she had returned to her room, donned a cool tunic of primrose embroidered cotton and taken as much time as she could over her make-up and hair, she was still unwilling to join everyone in the lounge until the last possible moment before it became a case of someone being sent to see why she hadn't yet put in an appearance.

As it was she felt like a stranger in her own home when she paused on the threshhold of the room before entering. She had become used to seeing her brother outnumbered by females in the homestead, but this evening the position had been reversed, and with a peculiarly unnerving effect. It was almost as if she was seeing their three guests for the first time and, unbidden, Lori's 'intensely masculine' definition sprang disturbingly into her mind. In form and feature they were very alike; sharing the same dark curling hair, the same upright and self-assured bearing, and the same powerful physiques. It was only in their eyes that they were totally diverse, and never had Ashley been more conscious of the fact than when each of them turned to watch her entry after Bruce had called out to ask what she wanted to drink.

The blue of Hal's was a twinkling encouragement, and Leigh's an amiable grey, but Dane's startling green set in such a deeply tanned face were the ones which riveted her gaze. At the moment they most resembled a winter ocean— cold and ominous—and she knew for a certainty that Hal's warning had been justified. For her own sake, it would be advisable not to crowd Dane too closely until that explosive tautness had left his body and the intimidating savagery his eyes! Clearing her throat nervously, she dragged her glance away to smile shakily at her brother and requested a Cinzano.

Dinner was even more of an ordeal when Ashley found Dane was seated directly opposite her at the long polished walnut table, although there was some comfort to be gained from having Hal occupying one of the places beside her, but it was impossible to continually keep her head turned to her left, and especially when the conversation taking place at the table was of interest to them all.

'So you've completely re-fenced the boundary with Bill-ambang,' said Bruce sociably soon after the meal had commenced and bringing a short nod from Dane in response.

'It was certainly due for it,' he elaborated, unnecessarily to Ashley's mind, and her eyes flicked up to his balefully, but lowered them to her plate just as quickly on encountering his narrowed and anticipatory gaze, refusing to give him another opportunity to belittle her management by censuring his remark.

'Those internal fences needing new wire can be done gradually, the boundaries are the most important, naturally,' Dane continued, his glance moving back to Bruce. 'Apart from causing annoyance and creating extra work for neighbours, it's a waste of time to have to keep chasing or returning straying stock.'

Didn't she know it! Ashley grimaced but said nothing, and it was Janelle who had the next comment to make.

'Leigh tells me you've got machinery coming in next week to build an air-strip. Do you fly your own plane too?' she quizzed interestedly.

He nodded. 'It's the quickest and most economical way of keeping an eye on everything when the distances between properties are so great.'

'And will you also go ahead and put in a couple more ground tanks like you said you were thinking of doing?' Leigh himself now enquired.

Outwardly nonchalant, Ashley went on cutting her roast lamb, but with all her senses on the alert. Perhaps not surprisingly, this was the first she had heard of either plan and she was determined not to miss the chance to glean whatever she could from the conversation.

'Mmm, probably, while the equipment's out here. Additional water never goes amiss,' Dane affirmed the query.

'Providing it does rain again, of course,' laughed Hal.

'It will,' came the confident prediction, 'and, let's hope, before too long. The weather patterns are starting to show a slight change.'

Ashley couldn't hold her silence any longer. 'They've done *that* before, and all we ever got out of it was a load of dry storms,' she informed him scornfully.

Dane's eyes clinically dissected her piece by piece. 'Then

they obviously weren't the *right* changes, were they?' he dismissed her dissidence peremptorily.

Positive her face was a crimson flag bright enough to draw everyone's attention to her humiliation, Ashley recoiled from his hostility and murmured a defensive but unsteady, 'Apparently not,' before resuming an undivided concentration on the food before her and leaving him with only a view of the top of her golden head and the dark shadows of her lashes as they closed over dispirited blue eyes. Why hadn't she kept her mouth shut as she had originally intended?

Hal came to the rescue before the lull which followed could become a tension-packed abyss. 'And the builders? You'll want them out as soon as possible too, I suppose, to make certain everything's back in place before the rains do come?'

For a time it seemed as if Dane wasn't going to answer, so intent was he on surveying Ashley's downbent head, but when it became evident she wouldn't be lifting her gaze to his again he expelled a heavy breath and gave his attention to his brother.

'Yes, I've arranged to meet Skinner here early tomorrow morning so he can have a look over the place and work out the best way of tackling the job.'

'You mean ... old man Skinner?' Hal gasped incredulously, then in a grating tone Ashley had never heard him use before, 'Or that mongrel of a son of his?'

'I should be careful what you say, if I were you, Hal,' he was advised with a sardonic grin. 'I understand Ashley and Ralph Skinner have been very—er—friendly for some time now.'

There was too much innuendo conveyed by that purposeful pause for Ashley to ignore it, although she did disregard Hal's expostulated, 'Ashley and *Ralph*! You've got to be kidding!' because she was determinedly holding Dane's glittering emerald gaze with a sweetly smug blue one.

'Which just proves how out of date your second-hand information is,' she smiled up at him, deliberately provocative. 'I haven't spoken to Ralph Skinner for weeks!' A slight exaggeration admittedly, but it was worth it in order to prove him wrong.

'Well, I'm glad to see you finally came to your senses,' Bruce unexpectedly put in from the far end of the table. 'Did you make some enquiries and find out what Alec and I said was true? That it was Ralph and not Dane who was the school bully?' Which was rewarded with an absolutely furious glare from Ashley and an extremely interested assessment from everyone else.

With no other choice open to her but to reply, Ashley did so as briefly as she could. 'Yes,' she half shrugged, hoping to pass the matter off, but unwittingly it was Hal who was to thwart her efforts with his disparaging demand,

'And just who was the idiot dumb enough to suggest otherwise in the first place?'

'Ashley!' pealed Janelle as she and the other two members of her family couldn't restrain their laughter at the look of despairing resignation on her face for the disclosure which promptly made her the cynosure of all amused eyes.

'But . . . why?' laughed Hal, though puzzled nonetheless.

'Oh, it wasn't altogether Ashley's fault.' Bruce realised what he had inadvertently started and tried to make amends. 'Ralph had spun her some fanciful tale and . . .'

'Why wouldn't I believe it? You always used to bully *me*!' Ashley decided to take a hand in her own defence and faced Dane accusingly across the table. 'You still do!' she added, intending it as a reproof but cursing mutely when her shaking voice turned it into a plaintive wail which set them all laughing once again.

But it was Dane's amusement which brought about her final, inescapable downfall. When his lips and eyes smiled at her with such breathtaking appeal she had no defences against him at all, and in sudden confusion she pushed back her chair and rose agitatedly to her feet.

'I—I think I'll go and see to the dessert,' she grabbed at the first excuse she could think of.

'But Nellie's already in the kitchen attending to that, dear,' her mother smiled gently.

Oh, heavens, she had to get out of here before she made a complete fool of herself! 'Then—then I'd better take my plate out,' she improvised in a panic, and picking up the fine bone china and silver cutlery from the table fled with them to the relative safety of the kitchen, the pounding of her heart threatening to suffocate her on the way.

CHAPTER SEVEN

ASHLEY wandered slowly back to the homestead, closing her eyes pleasurably and tilting her head back to allow the cool breezes to play over her flushed skin for the last time before pulling open the screen door and stepping on to the verandah.

She listened for the voices coming from the lounge and then turned away forlornly, trailing the tips of her fingers idly against the flymeshing as she walked. Her mother would probably have words to say about her rudeness in disappearing so swiftly after dinner when they had guests, but she would just have to accept that. It had been almost more than she could bear having to sit through the remainder of the meal under Dane's watchful eye, but when it came time for coffee she had whispered a hasty excuse in her mother's ear and had absented herself before another word could be spoken.

Nearing the doors which led into her bedroom she heard the unmistakable sound of footsteps behind her and she whirled round apprehensively, every nerve quivering as she saw Dane striding towards her.

'Ashley! Where the hell did you disappear to?' he forcefully shattered the cocoon of her external serenity.

If she thought she could have got away with it, she would have willingly run for her room and locked the doors against him. But as she couldn't imagine such a ploy defeating a man of Dane's determination, she merely tried to look surprised and lifted one shoulder impassively.

'I went for a walk, that's all,' she said. 'I often do.'

'Without waiting for your coffee?'

'Sometimes. It all depends what needs to be done.'

'But there was nothing that required your attention this evening,' he stated knowledgeably, subtly.

Ashley moved restlessly from one foot to the other. 'I—

why, old habits are hard to break, I guess,' she evaded huskily.

'Including trying to provoke me at every turn?' dryly.

She was glad the light was too dim for him to see the sudden rush of colour to her cheeks as she feigned ignorance by asking, 'Because I took a walk?'

A lazy smile showed the momentary flash of white teeth. 'Because you're doing it again, honey,' he drawled.

'I know, but I can't seem to help it. It just happens,' she abruptly found herself confessing to her amazement—and consternation.

'Maybe it does at that,' he smiled down at her so electrifyingly that Ashley could hardly breathe and dropped her eyes hurriedly. 'Although that wasn't what I wanted to talk to you about.' A finger under her chin brought her wary gaze back to his and he quizzed softly, 'Do you think it's possible for us to have a conversation for once without any fireworks?'

He sounded serious and Ashley tried to match his mood. 'I don't see why not. I'm not usually hard to get on with.'

'Good girl,' he grinned his approval and provided an inordinate rush of pleasure for his listener. 'Where can we sit?' as his glance swept along the chairless verandah.

'On the steps?' she offered tentatively. 'We did used to have some loungers and seats out here, but they gradually fell to pieces over the years and—and we didn't bother to replace them. There wasn't much time to use them anyway,' she shrugged, but feeling some sort of explanation was required.

'The steps it is, then.' Dane led the way, opening the door, and sharing one of the wide steps with her. 'Do you smoke?' he proffered a packet of cigarettes he had just taken from the pocket of his shirt.

Ashley shook her head. 'No, thanks.'

'Sensible,' he commended wryly as he put one between his own lips and applied the flame from a silver lighter.

'Not really,' she corrected with a half smile, strictly honest. 'I started once but couldn't afford to keep it up.'

Dane scrutinised the delicate features turned towards

him for a long time, until Ashley could feel a fiery warmth creeping under her golden skin and rapidly assumed an interest in the pattern of the embroidery covering her dress.

'You've had a hard time of it since your father died, haven't you, little one? You did the rags to riches bit in reverse.'

'I guess so,' she sighed, her lips forming a rueful moue as she recalled all the money her parent had wasted and all the expensive, but mainly useless, presents he had liked to buy. 'But I didn't really mind. Not as long as we still had ...'

'Kindyerra?'

Ashley chewed at her lip and retreated from the hurt such a thought was capable of producing. 'Is that what you wanted to talk to me about?' she avoided giving a direct answer.

As if sensing her reluctance to discuss the matter any further he obligingly shook his head. 'No, in actual fact, I wanted to know your opinion regarding some of the alterations I have in mind for the homestead. If you cast your mind back, you might remember I did mention it before, but you—um—left the office before we could get around to discussing them,' he reminded her lazily.

'But why my opinion?' she puzzled, valiantly striving to ignore the teasing note in his tone. 'Surely you would be better off consulting your—your ...' she had been going to say 'fiancée', but as she didn't know whether this was strictly correct as yet, and as she was having trouble forcing the word past her lips anyway, she finally substituted, '... your permanent housekeeper,' instead.

Dane gave her a level look of mocking patience. 'But I haven't yet employed a permanent housekeeper for Kindyerra and the builders are due to start work next week.'

'Then why not ask my mother, or—or Della?' she prompted grudgingly.

'Because I would rather Della didn't have a hand in it— that way the finished effect will be so much the greater— and because, when I mentioned it to your mother, she suggested that I should ask you as, in her words, "Ashley has a great feel for the place and she used to have quite a few plans of her own which she intended to put into practice if we ever managed to get that far ahead",' he relayed quietly, significantly.

Ashley's eyes sparkled rebelliously as a result of that disclosure. But none of those plans had been meant for Della Marchant's benefit! If she'd had any doubts as to whom Dane was intending to share Kindyerra with, she certainly had none now—his opening remark had all too plainly seen to that!

'Well?'

The somewhat tense demand for her attention brought Ashley out of her unpleasant reverie with a grimaced, 'I scrapped them.'

'But you can still remember what they were!' It was a categorical statement and in no way meant as a question.

'I'm not sure,' she began evasively, but on seeing the darkening look entering his eyes was prompted to concede halfheartedly, 'There could still be a couple of rough sketches hidden away in the office somewhere.'

'Good.'

Dane stubbed out his cigarette, caught hold of one of her hands and had them both on their feet and heading for the office before Ashley fully realised what was happening, although it didn't take her as long to become nervously aware that his fingers were still possessively interlaced with hers and immediately pulled away from the inflammable touch. With a studied effort she might have been able to attempt a civil conversation, but to accept any kind of physical contact was totally out of the question.

While Ashley began her cursory search through the filing cabinet, Dane assumed his usual position on the edge of the desk; one long leg swinging idly, one hand resting on his hip, his eyes watching her progress with deceptive indolence.

'How long were you dating Ralph?' he asked suddenly, angrily almost to Ashley's ears.

Her fingers still momentarily and then continued a little

faster than before. 'About six months,' she replied, purposely not turning to look at him.

'And you broke it off for the reasons Bruce mentioned?'

A deep breath and she slammed one drawer shut and dragged open the next violently. 'Partly . . . I never did like bullies!' she just had to gibe at the files in front of her.

To her surprise Dane laughed. 'And I'd hazard a guess and say the rebuff didn't sit too well on him either.' The amused speculation curled around her ironically.

'Does it with anyone? Or perhaps, being so superior yourself, you've never had to experience the feeling!' she rounded at last to query with a wide-eyed facetiousness she hadn't a hope of controlling.

He tut-tutted aggravatingly. 'Now, how could that be possible with you around to make sure it's otherwise?' he mocked so ruefully she had to spin back to her search in order to nullify the effect of his accompanying grin.

'As if you care what I say!'

'Don't sound so wistful,' he taunted impenitently. 'I might be persuaded into thinking you're disappointed.'

'How could I be?' she retorted, her skin burning with embarrassment at the implications inherent in his unfortunately accurate premise. 'As far as I'm concerned, there's very little difference between you . . . or Ralph!'

One corner of his mouth quirked upwards. 'Then try saving some of your antipathy for him too while he's here, hmm?'

'Ralph's coming here?'

'Didn't you know? His father's putting him in charge of the renovations.'

The idea was decidedly unattractive, but Ashley dismissed it impatiently and gave him a calculating glance from beneath thickly fringed lashes. 'And how do you feel about that?' she probed, interested in spite of herself.

His shoulders lifted unconcernedly. 'Unlike you, honey, I'm quite capable of controlling my animosities when I wish to. Provided he does a good job he'll strike no opposition from me.'

'And if he doesn't, what will you do? Beat him up again?' she goaded flippantly in an effort to strike back for his disparaging remark.

'You heard about that, did you?' he grinned wryly. 'However, if there's any fighting to be done I should imagine it will be restricted to a battle of words only. Resorting to a brawl very rarely accomplishes anything of value, and Ralph really doesn't look as if he has the condition to fight his way out of a paper bag these days, anyway.'

After a judicious moment spent comparing Dane's hard muscularity with the recalled softly deteriorating form of Ralph which had been so noticeable the last time they had gone out together, an irrepressible bubble of laughter rose in Ashley's throat in view of their parallel observations.

'I know,' she chuckled infectiously. 'I rather think he's enjoying the good life just a little too much for his own good of late.'

Dane's responding smile and the appreciative glint contained in his fascinating green eyes held Ashley spellbound —so much so in fact that she felt her legs were becoming alarmingly weak, and her breath to be almost choking her in its desire for release. Only when his hand reached out to enfold the back of her neck and pull her unresistingly closer did her instincts reassert themselves and she jerked feverishly away from him.

'I think I—I've found the sketches,' she burst out shakily in defence of an insurmountable feeling of vulnerability, her fingers scrabbling among the folders in the drawer and bringing forth three small sheets of somewhat crumpled paper. 'I threw them away once and then resurrected them —that's why they're a bit crinkled,' she half laughed nervously as she attempted to flatten out more of the creases before handing them to him, eyes determinedly downcast all the while.

A hand beneath her chin soon altered that, however, and her gaze was unwillingly made to meet his yet again. 'My God, but you're a jittery little bundle tonight, honey,' he teased with a laugh. 'What did you think I was going to do?'

'I ... does it matter?' Ashley shifted restively under his gaze, positive her face was scarlet, and desperately sought a change of subject by reproaching, 'I thought the whole idea of coming in here was to discuss the renovations.'

'So it was,' Dane concurred smoothly. 'But somewhere along the way I seem to have developed the habit of allowing you to sidetrack me.' He rubbed a hand around the back of his neck, sounding considerably more rueful than cheerful over the acknowledgment, noted Ashley despondently. 'Come on then, let's have a look at these drawing of yours and see if they tie in with any of my plans.'

Seated at the desk, Ashley laid the sheets of paper out before her, including the neatly drawn layouts Dane had withdrawn from his hip pocket before leaving to borrow a long-legged stool from the kitchen. Returning a few minutes later he lowered his length on to it close beside her chair and leant forward to peruse the sketches carefully, his bronzed forearms resting on the desk, his shoulder touching hers disturbingly.

Fortunately, her quickening interest in his designs for the homestead soon overcame her disquiet at his proximity and she found herself discussing every aspect of the reconstructions with a surprising candour and spontaneity. Some of his ideas coincided with her own and some were vastly different, but it was patently clear all the same that the building was about to receive the face-lift of a lifetime and would never be recognisable—even in shape—as the same slightly shabby dwelling it had gradually become since her father's purchase eighteen years before.

Each bedroom was to have its own bathroom—a veritable boon considering how long Janelle was spending in their one and only these days—and air-conditioning incorporated throughout. The lounge would be expanded to almost three times its present size, and new dining and family rooms added. The kitchen completely remodelled and every time-saving device imaginable installed, the verandahs extended to fifteen feet for extra shade. Even the office was to receive attention, the location being changed to the back of the homestead and then enlarged, with the wry comment, 'So there's room for more than one chair.'

Dane turned his head to look at her, his face only inches away. 'Well, what do you think of it?' he smiled.

Ashley swallowed hard and eased back in her chair in order to put a little more distance between them as much as anything. 'It's quite ... staggering!' she owned, impressed, before continuing with a sardonic, 'and so's what it will cost.' Especially when consideration was given to all the other improvements which were to take place to the station itself!

'More than likely,' he grinned lazily. 'But I figure it's worth it. Efficiency improves out of sight when you're working with good reliable equipment.'

'On the property, yes!' Ashley couldn't have agreed more. 'But surely there isn't the same need to go to quite so much trouble with the homestead?'

'Why not? It's as important to be able to relax in pleasant surroundings as it is to work in them. Besides,' he eyed her with a slight tinge of mockery, 'don't you consider a housekeeper, or wife, is as entitled to the same modern conveniences inside the house as her employer, or husband, is outside it?'

Of course, she had temporarily forgotten that all these developments were being made on Della's behalf! Now the distasteful remembrance returned in full force and the cornflower blue of her eyes deepened with sarcasm.

'Naturally I do! As long as money's no object, of course!' she flared.

The firm outline of his jaw was abruptly more apparent. 'You had your chances, Ashley, the same as I did! The only difference was ... you blew yours!' he retaliated coolly.

'The same chances you had ...!' she repeated incredulously. 'I inherited a damned great mortgage with this place when my father died! What did you get with the first piece of land you bought, Dane?'

'An unencumbered, well managed, and well stocked property,' he divulged with an unexpected but wholly disarming smile, all traces of his previous derision disappearing as his expression turned strangely indulgent. 'Okay, honey, I'll admit you came into the business the hard way, and you were very young to take on such a responsibility, even though you had plenty of experienced staff at the time. But,' his explicit pause gave the word an incredible emphasis, 'in turn, I expect you to admit that the state of affairs which finally brought about the sale of Kindyerra resulted solely from *your* mistakes!'

'Mis*take*! There was only one,' she amended immediately, but without her former belligerence in view of his placatory remarks.

'That's all it takes when they're of that magnitude,' dryly.

Ashley pulled a flippant face. 'Advice from the infallible?' she quipped.

'Uh-uh! Everyone makes errors, including myself,' he drawled. 'I just make certain that any doubtful decisions I do make can be easily rectified if I'm proven wrong, and aren't those which could jeopardise any of my investments as a whole. When you've just spent four or five years building up a decent flock—with all the expenditure and hard work that involves—you don't gamble with your investment, honey, you protect it! With the outstanding debts the property was already carrying, you must have known when you decided against sending them away that you wouldn't be getting another chance if the decision was the wrong one.'

'But I talked it over for hours with Ted,' she protested. 'And you can't say he doesn't know what he's doing with stock.'

'I agree, there's none better ... with stock!' he stated unequivocally. 'That's just the point—it's not husbandry we're discussing, it's management!'

Her management, or mismanagement, thought Ashley glumly. It was too morbid to dwell upon and she deliberately dismissed it with a shrug.

'Oh, well, it's all water under the bridge now—although I rather think that was the wrong proverb to use under the circumstances,' in wry musing. 'At least it presented you with the opportunity to regain Kindyerra and do all this,' indicating the drawings still lying on the desk. 'Which reminds me of a question I had intended to ask earlier. Why did you choose the Skinners for the alterations, Dane? All things considered, I would have thought you'd have preferred to ...'

'Take my business elsewhere?' he finished helpfully, then shook his head. 'As much as I may dislike the family personally, I'm still willing to give credit where it's due. Ralph Skinner, senior, is a first class tradesman who won't tolerate any shoddy workmanship from his employees ...'

'For which he charges accordingly,' Ashley inserted effervescently.

'As he has always done,' Dane gave a responding smile. 'But I'm prepared to pay his prices in order to have the work carried out to my satisfaction.'

'You aren't worried he might be tempted to ... overcharge you?' From remarks Ralph had sometimes unwittingly let fall it evidently wasn't unknown for them to try.

'Do you think it's likely?'

He'd be a fool if he did, she decided pungently. And on second thoughts she couldn't really see Ralph's father trying anything of that kind on a man of Dane's character— he was too wily an old bird for that—but his son was something else, the more so since she doubted Ralph would be prepared to restrain his hostilities as Dane had declared he was.

'I don't think Mr Skinner would,' she finally let him slowly into her thoughts. 'But Ralph—you're not exactly his favourite person, you know.'

'Yours either,' he reminded her lazily. 'So how do you think we're going to get along living under the same roof for the next few months?'

Ashley blinked in astonishment, suddenly imbalanced, and not only by his statement but by his rapid change of topic as well.

'That all depends on exactly what you mean by "living under the same roof",' she frowned warily.

'Your mother has invited Hal and myself to join Leigh in moving across here to save the unnecessary travelling.'

Momentarily Ashley's eyes closed in despair. Oh, hell, what did you have to go and do that for? she reproached her mother mutely. As if it wasn't already hard enough to keep her feelings submerged without having him a constant reminder as to how frail her defences really were! On a slowly exhaled breath she compelled herself to shrug unworriedly.

'When it becomes too unbearable, I'll let you know.'

One eyebrow rose mockingly. 'You surprise me. I was under the impression you'd find it that right from the beginning.'

Damn! She was obviously allowing this conversation to become a shade too amiable. In an effort to counter the situation Ashley strove to inject just the right amount of provocation into her voice.

'And is that what you were hoping for? Protests from me which you could contemptuously reject because, to all intents and purposes, this property is yours now and it's only due to your charitable benevolence that we're allowed to remain at all?' she gibed deliberately. 'Well, I'm sorry if I've caused a disappointment by depriving you of some amusement at my expense. You'll just have to hope for better results next time, won't you?'

'Where you're concerned I doubt it's possible for anything to get better,' Dane returned icily, his eyes narrowing as they raked over her defiantly angled face. 'As for you disappointing me ... you started off as the most insolent brat imaginable, and you've grown into the most belligerent virago I've ever met, so how could I be disillusioned? It's necessary to have at least *some* faith in a person before they can fall short of your expectations!' he laughed so derogatorily that Ashley actually winced.

'And you started out as the most objectionable bully imaginable, and you've grown into the most arrogant pig I've ever met!' she hurled back at him in similarly denigrating terms, the anger she had been simulating now becoming a blazing reality as she whirled out of the chair and around to the front of the desk where her hands rested flat on its surface and she leant slightly forward to taunt, 'But you needn't think you've got me cornered with all those threats of yours regarding bankruptcy if I don't conform with that clause you saw fit to insert in the contract! I don't mind waiting for the right moment—like, when the builders are halfway through the renovations—to pack my bags and walk out of here and away from your damned harassment! Then we'll see just how well your intimidations hold good, won't we?' with a pertly superior smile.

Not that it was permitted to last long, for Dane came off the stool, reached across the desk and gripped her wrist painfully, and had pulled her roughly towards him before she even had a chance to head for the door.

'I wouldn't be too confident of that if I were you!' He was so close Ashley could see her own apprehensive reflection in the freezing depths of his eyes as his fingers dug significantly deeper into her skin, bringing involuntary tears to hide her image behind a misty veil. 'You're deluding yourself if you believe I was witless enough to have laid all my cards on the table, honey!'

'Meaning?' she whispered throatily.

'I'm hardly likely to tell you, am I? That would defeat the purpose entirely,' he smiled scornfully, hatefully. 'All you need to know is that I don't make idle threats—and I don't bluff!'

Ashley nodded weakly and to her relief it appeared to suffice, because he finally released her and resumed his seat, enabling her to rub some life back into her numbed extremity as she turned on her heel and hurried for the door.

'Ashley!'

She swung round, half wary, half defiant, her lashes dark and wet. 'Yes?'

'I'm sorry if I hurt your wrist,' he apologised curtly.

'And I'd say, "It doesn't matter," if I thought you meant it,' was the bitter retort as she about-turned again and continued on her way with a rueful sniff. So much for civil conversations!

Although it probably wasn't the best of times to have extra people in the homestead, Ruth Beaumont was obviously in her element with so many to care for, and had any of the workmen wished to stay overnight she would have welcomed them with open arms too. Having been an only child herself she loved it best when she was surrounded by her family, and as she had always had a soft spot for the Carmichaels she had accepted and was treating them as her own before the week was out.

Janelle, of course, was in the seventh heaven with Leigh a permanent companion when she returned from work each day, and Bruce was clearly pleased to have some male company with whom he could discuss his mechanics for a change. But Ashley spoke only enough to prevent it becoming glaringly noticeable that she wasn't as at ease as she should be, and that she was deliberately refraining from participating in most of the verbal exchanges. Oh, she shared a joke occasionally with Hal or Leigh, and her behaviour towards the members of her family differed only slightly from normal, but when it came to Dane she maintained a stony, protective silence which she refused to break unless it was absolutely imperative that she do so.

It was a new approach to her ever-present problem—how to combat a magnetism which seemed to be growing daily, and yet conceal her own turbulent emotions at the same time. If she couldn't have Dane's love then she would rather accept hate in lieu of pity—or worse, amusement—should he ever discover that her whole attitude was one great pretence undertaken solely for self-preservation.

Dane's reaction to her change of disposition was difficult to define. On occasion Ashley could have sworn he was on the verge of taking to her physically, so infuriated were his expressions, but in other instances he appeared to find considerable humour in the situation—as if he knew exactly what was going through her mind—and which, of course, had her doubling her efforts to prove him mistaken.

And she might even have been able to continue in this relatively composed fashion for some time if it hadn't been for Ralph Skinner. During the first week that the carpenters were making their presence felt at the homestead his father had been out there to make certain everything got under way correctly, but by the middle of the following week Ralph arrived—almost visibly pleased with his own importance—and after having openly ignored Ashley for most of the day, eventually sauntered along the verandah to the office late in the afternoon, and without waiting to be invited he walked straight into the room as if he owned it, looking about him contemptuously.

'So this is the poky little rabbit hutch where all the big decisions are made. I'm not surprised he wants a bigger one,' was his initial deprecation.

Ashley closed the ledger she had been working on and eyed him with distaste, wondering just how she could have endured his company for the length of time she had. Or perhaps she had only managed to because she'd had so many other problems to worry over during that period that she really hadn't been paying as much attention as she should. Now her head lifted angrily at his derisive remarks which were quite uncalled for in her view, and not altogether truthful anyway. The office might have been small, but it definitely was not 'poky'.

'Did you want to see me about anything in particular, Ralph? Or have you just come to be rude about things in general?' she enquired sarcastically.

'Oh, we are cute today, aren't we?' he sneered, his blue eyes glittering with a perturbing malevolence. 'I suppose through living in such close proximity with the lordly Carmichaels some of their condescension has rubbed off!'

'No, I'd rather take full credit for that myself,' she retorted. 'I don't really feel I need to borrow mannerisms from anyone in order to underestimate you.'

Ralph's lips thinned unpleasantly and he snorted, 'Look who's talking! From what I hear, the great man himself isn't exactly sold on you either, sweetie! Even though you have been generously sharing yourself around from the moment they arrived.'

'And just what's that supposed to mean?'

'Come off it, Ashley, you're not fooling me by playing dumb! You were seen at Della's party.'

'Dancing?' mockingly.

'No! Creeping outside for a nice quiet interlude with Hal, and then exchanging partners and carrying on with Dane!' he imparted his information with a jeer. 'What are you trying to do, share your favours between the whole family so you can compare them before deciding which one's the most proficient and which one you fancy best?'

Ashley spared a short moment to wonder whose fertile imagination had chosen to put such a deprecating construction upon her actions, and then she was on her feet and staring at him derogatorily.

'Get your mind up out of the dirt, Ralph!' he was advised with stinging contempt. 'You're becoming a nauseating bore!'

'Well, isn't that too bad!' his eyes ran over her insolently. 'But I notice you didn't deny it.'

'Why would I? I'm sure you have no intention of believing anything I might say to the contrary,' she lifted one shoulder indifferently and turned her back on him to begin rifling through the papers stacked on one of the shelves for a particular sales catalogue she needed, and hoping he would take the hint and leave.

He didn't, though—Ralph wasn't that considerate. Instead he clamped his hands on to her arms and pushed her back against the filing cabinet, his furious face menacingly close.

'You brazen little bitch!' he snarled. 'Don't think you can brush me off as if I was some form of annoying insect which needs exterminating just because the Carmichaels are lowering themselves to take what you're offering!'

'How dare you!' Ashley blazed, struggling fiercely to break his grip. 'I wouldn't stoop so low as to soil my hands by *brushing* you off! All I'd do is squash you under my heel like the repulsive slug you are!' she slated witheringly.

Only the sound of someone coughing meaningfully halted Ralph's next attack—and Ashley couldn't be sure it would have been a verbal one—and both their heads turned in unison as Dane walked calmly across the room, found the catalogue Ashley had been searching for and, incredibly, prepared to depart again without having uttered a single word.

'*Dane!*' It was a reproach, a plea, and an almost tearful surrender of her principles all at the same time.

He swung round casually at the doorway, dark brows lifted in interrogation. 'Mmm?'

Ashley's eyes fell before the irony in his and she knew he was doing it on purpose, in retaliation for her silent opposition. If she wanted his help she was going to have to ask him for it—he wouldn't be volunteering!

'Please . . .!' she murmured huskily, her gaze returning to his in defeat.

To her immense relief he paced back into the room and fixed Ralph with an unbelievably grim stare. 'At a guess, I'd say your presence was unwelcome, Skinner!' he began sardonically.

'And I'd say it was none of your business!' Ralph countered without lessening his hold on Ashley in the slightest. 'This is a personal matter, so why don't you just keep on going like you were planning to originally, hmm?'

With a nervously indrawn gasp Ashley watched the anger seeping into Dane's expression as he rasped, 'Because I've just made it my business too! And because I have no intention of permitting you to conduct any of your affairs— personal or otherwise—in my office, on my property, and on my time! So I would suggest you take your hands off her —*right now*—and get yourself outside where you're supposed to be, before I damn well throw you out there!'

At last feeling Ralph's hold beginning to loosen, Ashley jerked herself quickly out of reach and moved closer to Dane's sheltering strength, profoundly grateful when his arm caught her safe against his side.

As he had sauntered into the office, so Ralph now sauntered out of it. 'There's no need to become violent,' he half laughed sarcastically, but endeavouring to stay out of Dane's range for all that, Ashley noted. 'Personally, I wouldn't consider her worth fighting over, but there's no accounting for taste, is there?'

'Pig!' Ashley muttered darkly after his departing figure.

'Thanks!'

She glanced upwards, perplexed. 'For what?'

'For putting me in the same category as Ralph. The last time you were actually talking to me that's also what you reckoned I was,' he recalled dryly.

'I'm sorry,' she apologised with a smile, a large proportion of her happiness being attributable to Ralph's exit. 'But thank you for—for your help. I thought you meant to leave me to my fate, at first,' as she half turned and shyly went up on to her toes so that she could place a light kiss at the corner of his mouth.

Dane had her imprisoned against his chest and a hand tilting her head to his without any effort. 'And if that's all the gratitude it was worth, maybe I should have done,' he threatened, and leisurely proceeded to exact his own fee with an irresistibly hungry kiss which had Ashley melting against his rugged shape and responding unconditionally.

When he eventually raised his head, it was to shake it ruefully. 'That's the second time I've almost been involved in a scrap because of you, honey. First Hal, and now Ralph. There must be something about you which brings out the worst—and the best—in a man.'

'I'm sorry,' she dropped her glance uncomfortably to the region of his chest. 'I make it awkward for everyone, don't I?'

'Damned awkward!' he agreed with wry feeling as he bent to retrieve the catalogue which had fallen unheeded to the floor moments earlier, rolled it and touched it to his forehead in a casual salute. 'Think about it,' he urged half seriously as he left her to stand staring after him with a thoughtful frown.

CHAPTER EIGHT

IN the hot dry weeks which followed, Ashley often did find herself thinking about that cryptic remark. Most times she managed to convince herself that he had meant it as a rebuke—an indirect reference that he found his involvement embarrassing in view of his relationship with Della. But that still left his kisses to explain away. If he was planning to marry Della, then why did he keep kissing her? Unless it was just one of those disconcerting means of his to keep her unbalanced and simultaneously enjoy a last fling! She could imagine that Dane wouldn't be a man to forsake his bachelorhood lightly, and perhaps he had only lately become aware how close its approaching demise actually was.

Today had been one of those sweltering days when the temperature climbed swiftly and persistently since early morning and the stillness was so complete it was as if every living creature was waiting breathlessly for some earth-shaking event to occur. There wasn't an insect or a bird making a sound, and since lunch even the dogs hadn't bothered to take their cooling dips in the horse trough any more, preferring to sprawl in whatever shade they could find to watch and wait, their sides heaving rhythmically.

In the oppressively silent atmosphere it was easy to pick up the muted drumming of a vehicle and with a grateful sigh for the interruption to her sorting of unwanted material in preparation for their move to the new office the following day, Ashley fanned a hopefully breeze-creating hand in front of her face and stood in the doorway to watch the white Chrysler make its approach in a cloud of billowing red dust.

Apparently Della wasn't prepared to wait for Dane to give the go-ahead for her to view the alterations—she wanted a preview now! Fleetingly, Ashley was tempted to retreat out of sight and allow her mother the joy of greeting their visitor, but as the car was now crossing the last grid and sweeping up to the homestead she considered it might be a little late for such a desertion, for it was more than likely that her mulberry printed sun-dress had already been noticed.

Carefully making her way down a set of makeshift steps —the original verandah had now disappeared into the extension and the new boards hadn't as yet been fastened into place—Ashley was surprised to hear Ramsay Marchant's voice calling a greeting, because she hadn't realised there were two persons in the sedan.

'Hello there, lass. My word, but they're getting a move on, aren't they?' he applauded as he took in the changes already made. 'You won't know the place when it's finished.'

'Which, no doubt, is exactly what Dane had in mind when he decided to make them,' drawled Della silkily after sharing the briefest of acknowledgments with Ashley.

A slightly brighter sparkle in her eyes was the only indication of Ashley's feelings as she determinedly ignored the remark and replied to the elder Marchant.

'Yes, it has changed, hasn't it?' she smiled warmly. 'And even more so inside, except that at the moment most of it's still in the disorderly stage and you need to watch where you're walking if you don't want to come to grief,' with a rueful laugh of experience.

'Then perhaps this wasn't a convenient time to come?' Ramsay immediately responded with concern.

'Oh, for goodness' sake, Father, don't let Ashley put you off,' his daughter called imperiously over one shoulder as she forged on ahead. 'If you suggested we came some time in the future she'd probably say all the paint was wet, or something! Besides, it belongs to Dane now—it's not up to Ashley to give her approval or otherwise any more.'

A speaking glance at the older girl's back and Ashley turned to Ramsay to explain hastily, 'I wasn't really objecting to your coming, but I did think it only fair to warn you of what to expect.'

'I know, Ashley, I know,' he smiled down at her reassur-

ingly. 'And I apologise for my daughter's thoughtless remarks concerning Dane's ownership. I think she's finding it
a little dull with only myself for company now that he and
his brothers have moved over here permanently, and the
time it's taking to get everything settled for her move is
making her somewhat irritable,' he excused Della's behaviour soothingly.

Ashley hadn't realised Della ever needed a reason to be
difficult or disdainful, but considerately refrained from saying so, merely nodding her head in supposed understanding
of his comments and directing Ramsay around the side of
the house towards the steps at the rear.

'You might find it easier if you go in through the back
door, Della,' she felt obliged to point out a few moments
later as the other girl prepared to walk across the loose
boards which would form part of the new verandah when it
was completed.

In her desire to deliver a caustic, 'But as *I* don't happen
to be an employee, I'll use the *front* door, thank you,
Ashley!' Della unfortunately forgot to look where she was
treading, with the result that she missed her step and one
foot slid between two separating boards accompanied by a
shriek of mixed pain and anger.

To make matters worse, before Ashley or Ramsay could
reach her, Bruiser, one of the cattle dogs who had chosen
that particular spot beneath the verandah for shade, now
bounded forward to sniff interestedly at the strange in-
truder to his domain.

'Get away from me, you damned mongrel!' Della shouted
as his wet nose trailed over her skin, and moved her foot
backwards as far as the wood allowed with obvious intent.

'Don't kick him!' Ashley commanded shrilly as she ran
forward, not because she had any fear of Della being able
to strike the dog, he was too used to dodging lashing
hooves for that, but because she knew the inevitable outcome such an action would bring forth.

Her warning came too late, however, or was disregarded,
for Della's foot thrust forward viciously at the inquisitive
nose and the next moment pandemonium broke loose as

Bruiser's training came to the fore and he dropped flat to the ground so that the foot flew harmlessly over his head, and then sank his teeth into the back of Della's leg in the same manner as he did with recalcitrant cattle.

Luckily a sharp whistle was all that was required from Ashley to have Bruiser releasing his victim and returning to her side, but with such a happily complacent look on his face she was hard put to smother a grin, and then Ramsay was helping his irate daughter to her feet as Ruth Beaumont came to the door to see what had caused all the commotion.

'That savage beast ought to be shot! Look what he's done to me!' Della screamed frenziedly, oblivious to her father's attempts at pacification.

'I'm very sorry, Della, but you shouldn't have tried to kick him. We had a stockman here once who did that to him as a pup and he's never forgotten it, I'm afraid,' Ashley defended the dog stoutly.

Sizing up the situation swiftly, Ruth came forward now to put a supporting arm around Della and help her into the house, murmuring gently about antiseptics and bandages as they went, while Ashley and Ramsay followed carefully across the verandah.

'I am sorry, Ramsay,' she apologised again to the man beside her, although unable not to secretly consider that Della really deserved what she'd received through attempting to kick the dog when he hadn't been doing her any harm. 'I hope his teeth didn't go too deep.'

'I don't expect so, he didn't have hold of her for that long,' he spoke encouragingly. 'Anyway, Della should have known better. I keep telling her to try and control that temper of hers—maybe this will serve as a lesson.' Unexpectedly his kindly eyes twinkled humorously. 'That's a fast moving dog you've got there. I don't suppose you'd consider selling him?'

Ashley laughed and shook her head. 'No, I'm afraid not. He's one of the best workers we have and I think Dane has ideas of mating him with that little red bitch of his.'

Ramsay only just had time to finish his meditative,

'Mmm, a promising combination. I'll have to see about buying one of the pups,' before Della's limp grew noticeably worse and she turned her head to snap,

'I'm glad you can find something to laugh about, Ashley! You might not think it quite so amusing, though, if that mongrel ravages your leg instead of mine next time.'

Ashley wouldn't have said 'ravage' was exactly the right description. The bite had been sharp and clean and there was hardly any blood about the puncture marks. She also considered pointing out that as she wasn't in the habit of kicking her dogs there was really very little likelihood of it happening to her. But for the sake of peace and quiet she offered a contrite, 'I'm sorry, Della. Is it very sore?' instead.

'Of course it's damned sore! Why else would I be limping so badly?'

Strongly tempted to retort with a sarcastic, 'For effect, naturally,' Ashley pressed her lips together tightly and thought it best not to answer at all. Evidently whatever she had to say was only going to make things worse, so while her mother took Della off to the bathroom she diplomatically stayed behind with Ramsay and showed him the difference which had been wrought in the kitchen as she set about making some tea.

'Good heavens! I wouldn't have believed it possible!' were his first stunned comments as he looked about him. 'What an improvement!'

'Mmm, it's that all right,' smiled Ashley wryly, and went on to explain unnecessarily, 'it still has to be painted, of course, but that won't be done until the rest of the alterations are completed.'

Ramsay nodded his understanding and wandered round the room to scrutinise everything more closely. 'Your mother will find it hard to leave all this behind when it comes time for her to leave,' he proposed discerningly.

'Yes—yes, I suppose she will.' It hadn't really occurred to Ashley before that being given the opportunity to see how well the homestead could look might make the final parting all that much more painful, and her own eyes scanned the room with new interest as she sighed a deep, 'I guess we all will.'

'And the sale is actually finalised now?' he enquired as he bent to inspect the double oven.

'Yes, the last of the exchanges were made a week ago,' flatly, diligently occupying herself by pouring the boiling water from the kettle into the teapot.

'Here we are!' Ruth smiled as she showed a bandaged Della into the room a few seconds later. 'I don't think there's any risk of infection—he didn't penetrate very deeply.' And as their visitor flounced huffily into a chair, 'What do you think of it, Ramsay?'

'Incredible, Ruth,' he smiled back. 'It must be the type of kitchen every woman dreams of having.'

'Well, I must say it's certainly revived my interest in the preparation of food. I haven't done so much home baking for years, have I, Ashley?' she sought her daughter's confirmation happily.

'You didn't exactly have the time for it either,' was the prompt but rueful reminder.

'Oh, well, that's the way it goes sometimes,' Ruth brushed aside thoughts of the bad years lightly. 'I certainly can't complain about a lack of time, or a lack of mouths to feed now. It's lovely to have so much company in the house.'

Ashley spread a lace cloth over the table and then placed the tray bearing the tea things on it. 'I'm sorry, but we'll have to have it in here. The lounge and dining room have been—er—otherwise engaged for a while now,' she smiled as the sound of hammering issued forth from that direction of the house.

'You mean you've all been eating your meals in the kitchen?' Della queried, managing to make it sound almost criminal.

'Except for those evenings when we've had barbecues,' supplied Ruth imperturbably as she began pouring the tea and Ashley passed out the cups. 'We could hardly keep moving the dining suite out of the workmen's way all the time, and I doubt it would be very pleasant to eat lunch with that noise in the same room,' dryly.

'Oh, in that case ...' Della half smiled ingratiatingly, suddenly aware that Mrs Beaumont wasn't quite as defence-less as she had always believed her to be, and that her father was eyeing her unusually grimly.

Deeming it a politic moment, Ashley offered a plate piled high with freshly baked cream sponge slices. 'Would any-one care for a cake?' she asked animatedly.

The remainder of the time taken for afternoon tea passed smoothly enough, but then Della insisted on being shown what had been done to the rest of the house and it was Ruth who elected Ashley to be the guide while Ramsey and herself continued with their conversation.

After a reproachful glance at her mother for being so generous at her expense, Ashley rose reluctantly to her feet and led the way into the hall, heading first for the bed-rooms and intending to work her way back through the rest of the rooms from there.

'Did Dane tell you he didn't want me to see it until it was all finished?' Della asked surprisingly, smugly, as she gazed cursorily about the first room they entered.

'He did mention something about it,' Ashley admitted cautiously, not wishing to discuss the subject, but wonder-ing why Della couldn't have contained her curiosity all the same.

'So what do you think he'll say when he finds I've been over today to have a look?'

This question was even more surprising than the last, but Ashley refused to let her amazement show and only hunched her shoulders negligently. 'How should I know? It's nothing to do with me.' She walked quickly towards the next room in an effort to complete their Cook's tour as soon as possible.

Della sauntered after her, a smirking expression on her face. 'That's right, you're only an employee here now, and he would hardly be likely to discuss his personal affairs with a mere domestic, would he?' she scoffed haughtily.

'As I don't happen to be a domestic, I wouldn't know

that either,' Ashley smiled back with as much seeming indifference as she could muster. She was damned if she was going to let Della get under her skin with her taunting remarks!

'Then what does he pay you for? It couldn't possibly be for anything to do with the running of the property. I mean, you've already shown what a hopeless failure you are in that direction.'

'In whose opinion?' Ashley rounded on her swiftly, her temper beginning to rise no matter how much she willed it not to.

'Why, in—in . . .' Della blustered, caught unprepared by the sudden demand, and jeering finally, 'Well, in mine for a start!'

'Which isn't a point of view I'm liable to lose any sleep over.' It was Ashley's turn to gibe now. 'After all, you wouldn't know the difference between a Merino, a Polwarth, or a Corriedale, unless someone pointed it out for you!'

The flush which covered Della's face nearly matched the colour of her hair. 'At least that's better than spending a day down at the yards and smelling like the damned greasy things for the next week!' she retaliated.

'In that case, I'd suggest you consider changing your brand of soap. Yours doesn't sound as if it works too well,' Ashley countered sardonically, and had bypassed two doorways before Della could catch up to her again. Just in time for Ralph to step out into the passage and deliberately block their way.

Unknowingly, Della proved to be an ally now by venting her anger on him instead. 'For heaven's sake, Ralph, stop standing there like some great over-fed statue and get out of our way!' she ordered in her most supercilious tone. 'If you've run out of work why don't you go and sharpen a chisel, or something, rather than make a nuisance of yourself!' as she pushed past him haughtily and made room for Ashley to do the same.

By the time Ralph had recovered from being so derisively put in his place, the two girls were already turning into the lounge where most of the building activity was taking place and, with an exaggerated wince in recognition of the noisy assault, Della protested sharply, 'Oh, I've had enough! I expected something better than this—this bedlam! It's not even interesting to look at,' with a grimace and stalked out into the hall.

Ashley shrugged offhandedly. It made no difference to her. Nevertheless, she couldn't help but think it strange that Della should have displayed such apathy when it was all being done in her honour. If anyone had gone to so much trouble and expense on Ashley's behalf, she would have been delirious! But perhaps Della's impassive reaction was only a front because it wasn't Dane who was showing her round, or maybe she was regretting the impetuosity which had driven her to ignore his wishes and come to look before it had been completed? Making her way back to the kitchen, Ashley sighed and shrugged again. Either way, it wasn't her concern.

Later, when Ramsay declared it was time they were leaving, and with no complaints from Della when they left by the rear steps, the air was so thick and heavy they felt as if they were forcing a passage through it.

Ramsay shaded his eyes and lifted them skywards to where the clouds were massing in ever larger formations. 'Looks like another storm is on its way,' he predicted conversationally.

'Wet or dry?' Ashley put in wryly.

'With the luck we've had for the past few years I'd have to say the latter,' he echoed her own thoughts on the matter.

Through having paid no attention to their remarks, Della's ears were the first to pick up an alien sound. 'Someone else is coming,' she announced.

'It's probably Dane and Leigh coming back from town,' Ruth surmised, accurately as it turned out once the vehicle became visible, and it wasn't long before it was being brought to a halt beside the Chrysler standing in the driveway.

'What a lovely surprise!' cooed Della sweetly, a smile

appearing for the first time that afternoon as she hobbled towards Dane with a limp that was worse now than it had ever been. 'You wouldn't believe the pains Ashley's taken to show me how the work's progressing and, of course, I approve ... except for one or two things I think could be improved upon.'

Dane's gaze when it locked with Ashley's conveyed his thoughts quite adequately without words, but as the blame for Della's viewing of the alterations had so unfairly been laid at her feet without her being accorded the chance to explain, she returned it with a challenging lift of her chin and an audacious widening of her deep blue eyes before turning to speak to Leigh as he joined them.

'Did you manage to get everything you wanted?' she asked.

Leigh nodded with satisfaction. 'Just about, although a couple of the parts for the windmill in Far East had to be ordered.' His hand dug into the hip pocket of his pants and came out with a bunch of roughly folded papers. Removing two he held them out to her. 'Here, you'd better keep these till they're ready to be collected. I'm likely to lose them otherwise,' he grinned.

Ashley slipped them into one of the square pockets of her dress, smiling, and turned back to the others when it appeared Ramsay and Della were preparing to leave. With their departure, and prior to the last trail of red dust settling back to earth, the conversation had automatically reverted to the weather.

'You reckon we'll get any rain out of it?' Leigh enquired of his brother after his eyes viewed the heavens narrowly against the brassy glare.

'I shouldn't think so,' the idea was discounted matter-of-factly. 'The clouds look too high to me.'

'Mmm, me too,' was the laconic agreement. Then curiously, as they headed for the house, 'What happened to Della's leg? Did she sprain it?'

'No. Apparently one of Ashley's dogs attacked her.'

'Oh!' Leigh looked down at Ashley interestedly. 'Why was that?'

'Because she tried to kick him!' she burst out resentfully. Della had certainly occupied her time well while she had been talking to Dane.

'Why would she do something like that?' Dane sounded mocking, as if he wasn't disposed to believing anything of the sort.

'Because he was sniffing at her foot after it had slipped between the boards on the front verandah!' she informed him witheringly.

Leigh's interpretation was, 'I suppose it gave him a fright and he bit first and looked afterwards,' but Ashley was swift to correct him with a decisive, 'No! He was only being inquisitive, but Della got mad and tried to boot him . . . and that's something Bruiser takes very strong exception to,' she added meaningfully.

'Then what was Della doing on the verandah in the first place?' Dane now demanded, but without giving any indication as to whether he finally believed her explanation or not, Ashley noted indignantly. 'Didn't you warn her about walking on those boards?'

'Of course I did!'

'Well . . .?'

'I was told that as she wasn't an employee—which I took to be a snide reference to myself—*she* would use the front door!'

There was a hastily smothered sound and then Leigh gave way to his laughter. 'Pride goes before a fall—literally—eh?' he grinned.

Dane's compelling mouth shaped lazily. 'Perhaps Ashley should take care in that respect too. I gather the demotion from employer to employee isn't one *her* pride finds easy to accept either,' he drawled.

As both her mother and Leigh were also attentively awaiting her answer to that little piece of deliberate baiting, Ashley determined not to be the one discomposed by it.

'But in my case it all depends on who's doing the employing. I had no objection at all to working for Tony Mancinelli,' she taunted with a provoking smile as she broke away from the group and made for the stairs to the office, intending to put away the sales slips Leigh had given her.

Among the boxes of accumulated material it took a little while to find the right receptacle for them and she had only just inserted them within the correct folder when Dane walked in behind her.

'I've got a little job for you ... if you have no objection, that is,' he delivered his remark with a slow smile, dropping some brightly coloured folders on to the desk. 'I picked up these charts in town because the painters will be wanting to know the colour schemes to be used fairly shortly. I thought you would be the best one to choose them.'

'Me?' Ashley blinked her surprise. 'But—but ...'

'Don't you think you can manage it?'

'Of course I can!' She had been going to ask if such a decision shouldn't have been left to Della, but had decided against it. Now she needed another reason for her hesitation and it wasn't hard to find. 'But what sort of colour schemes do you want? Light—dark—two-tone?'

'That's up to you, honey,' he laughed. 'I'm leaving it all in your capable hands.'

Seeing him already halfway back to the door she rushed agitatedly after him. 'But I still can't decide on any colours until I know what furnishings you intend using. I might select apricot walls in a room where you plan to have a purple carpet,' she proposed extravagantly.

'Then it looks as if it might be advisable for you to take charge of the floor coverings, etcetera, as well, doesn't it?'

The corners of Ashley's mouth curved ruefully. Somehow she had the feeling she'd been got at! 'You're sure you wouldn't like me to pick out the furniture for you while I'm about it too?' she quizzed mockingly.

His approving, 'Good idea,' was uttered so readily and with such a gratified smile that there were absolutely no doubts at all left in Ashley's mind that she had indeed been outmanoeuvred. This was what he had intended all along!

'But I'm not qualified to judge what will suit someone else's tastes,' she protested. 'You could object to the final result intensely!' Which was more than likely where Della was concerned, she decided wryly. Not in her wildest dreams could she imagine her choice pleasing that red-head.

Dane rejected her premise peremptorily. 'That's my look-out,' he smiled, unperturbed. 'You just go ahead and order whatever's necessary and send the accounts to me.' He caught her chin lightly between thumb and forefinger and his head lowered fractionally closer as he taunted, 'This time try to control your naturally defiant inclinations and refrain from giving Della a guided tour, though, as soon as my back's turned, hmm?'

'That's not fair!' Ashley pulled out of his hold and eyed him resentfully. 'I didn't invite her to come over, and she practically demanded to be shown what had been done. What was I supposed to do ... use myself as a human barrier to prevent her?'

'That's not the way I heard it.'

'So you automatically presume I'm the one who's not telling the truth!' she flared, hurt, but knowing it would never be different. 'In that case, I'm surprised you're letting me order everything for the homestead. Aren't you afraid I'll rob you blind in the process?' she gibed.

'If I was, I wouldn't have asked you to undertake it, so stop flying off at a tangent, you little firebrand, and calm down!' she was ordered as he raked an exasperated hand through his hair. 'Believe it or not, I don't need you to tell me that Della can be one hell of a determined female when she chooses.'

'Then why accuse me of arranging it behind your back?'

A lazily ironic smile made its appearance. 'Because, knowing how contrary *you* can be on occasion, honey, I thought it a distinct possibility,' he advised with a slight nod of his head as he continued on his way towards the outbuildings.

Strong words of repudiation rose to Ashley's lips, but were never voiced. In all honesty how could she refute his statement? She hadn't really been what could be called a fund of co-operation since Dane's return. For a second she stared pensively after his lithe figure and then started rapidly forward, preparing to overhaul him.

'I do wish you'd stop walking off before I've finished what I want to say,' she reproved after a hand laid briefly on his arm had successfully brought him to a halt, brows raising enquiringly, and his head shaking regretfully in response to her complaint.

'Sorry, little one, but there's a couple of matters I want to attend to before that storm hits.' His green eyes slanted upwards as if gauging how much time he had left, and then came to rest on her creamy-skinned features. 'What's on your mind?'

'It was about the furniture,' she lifted one shoulder detractingly, 'but I guess the other's more important so I can wait until later,' remembering her own concern on previous occasions.

'That might be best,' he agreed absently, his thoughts obviously on other things. 'I'll have a talk to you about it afterwards . . . okay?'

Ashley nodded her acquiescence and turned towards the homestead. After only a few steps she spun back again, tempted to offer her assistance. Then just as suddenly she shook her head and reversed direction once more. No! If she changed her attitude too much he was likely to become suspicious!

The family station wagon with Janelle at the wheel now came racing across the cattle grid, showering gravel in all directions as it sped along the drive, and Ashley waited at the corner of the house for her sister to join her after garaging the vehicle.

'The poor old car hasn't been pushed along that hard for years,' Janelle grinned impenitently, curls bouncing, as she hurriedly closed the gap between them. 'But I was scared stiff I was going to get caught in that!' with a finger pointing to the darkening sky above them and giving an expressive shudder. 'You know how I hate these wretched things!'

'Never mind,' Ashley smiled teasingly as they walked around to the back entrance and mounted the steps. 'You'll have Leigh to comfort you this time.'

'Uh-uh, no, I won't,' Janelle shook her head vigorously. 'It would be too embarrassing if he discovered how stupidly frightened they make me. I shall probably go straight to my room and stay there—hidden under the bed most likely—until it's all over,' she exaggerated with a wry grin.

Pulling open the screen door, Ashley laughed, 'You don't think he might consider your behaviour a little strange?'

'Better that than have him know the truth!'

The door clicked shut behind them and Ruth Beaumont looked up with a relieved smile. 'I'm glad to see you made it in time, Jan. Although I hope you didn't drive too fast on the way.'

'No, Mum,' Janelle looked at Ashley and winked conspiratorially. 'I was just lucky that I managed to get away from the salon early for once.'

'Yes, well, I expect everyone was anxious to get away this afternoon,' her mother accepted the explanation readily, but without taking her eyes from the new and decidedly complicated recipe she was following. 'If you'd like a cold drink there's some fruit juice in there,' waving a hand towards the fridge.

'Would I ever!' Janelle greeted the suggestion with heartfelt appreciation. 'The car was red hot when I got into it and there wasn't a breath of wind on the way home to help cool it down either.'

Taking three glasses from a cupboard, Ashley poured drinks for each of them, took a refreshing sip from her own, and glanced through the window at the pale orange light which was eerily illuminating the landscape. She moved one step closer and then involuntarily recoiled, her drink slopping wildly against the sides of the glass, as the same brilliant light blazed abruptly into the kitchen when the first of the awesome lightning streaks which typified a dry storm zig-zagged across the sky.

'Lord! That ... was ... close!' she emphasised each word dramatically and waited for the ensuing crack of thunder which had them all flinching away from its deafening stridency.

'Too close for mine, thanks very much!' Janelle half

laughed nervously as she placed her glass on the table. 'I think it's time I retired to my room and . . .' She broke off with a gasp as another jagged flare enveloped the nearby paddocks in blinding colour, then went on with a rush, 'I'll see you all later,' as she whirled out of the room with her hands pressed to her ears in readiness for the next jarring thunderclap.

Ashley watched her sister's departure with sympathetic eyes—Janelle had always hated storms—but not offering to keep her company because she knew from previous experience that the younger girl favoured seclusion at such times in order to confine her fearfulness to herself. It wasn't even as though Janelle hadn't made numerous attempts to control her fears, because she had, but to no avail, and much to her disgust she remained as nervous as ever.

The next brilliant illumination coincided with the men's entry into the kitchen, whereupon Bruce—newly released from the restrictions of his plaster—took one quick look over his shoulder and grinned, 'As Nellie always likes to say . . .'

'Him plurry big feller storm!' they all laughed in unison —everyone of them familiar with the much repeated quote —and Hal added a wry, 'At least we only have to keep an eye on the trees this time—I don't think there's a blade of grass left to catch fire!' as he handed out cold cans of beer from the fridge.

'Isn't that the truth!' Leigh nodded in agreement. 'The earth's so dry out there that some of the cracks are over a couple of inches wide.' He took a long mouthful of his drink and cast his eyes enquiringly round the room. 'Where's Jan? Isn't she home yet?' he asked with a slight frown.

Ruth closed the oven door on her ham and vegetable casserole and looked up with a smile. 'Yes, she's home— early today, as a matter of fact—but she's in her room at the moment. Probably getting ready for dinner,' she proposed, gently obstructive.

'I'd better not hold her up for too long, then,' Leigh returned cheerfully as he headed for the hallway, while

Ashley and her mother hunched their shoulders and exchanged helpless looks. He was bound to find out sooner or later!

'What was that all about?' probed Dane after Hal and Bruce had wandered out on to the side verandah to view the storm from closer quarters, and he had invited Ashley to join him in the lounge so they could resume their discussion concerning the homestead.

'Oh, nothing much,' she played dumb for her sister's sake and proceeded to pretend and absorbed interest in the construction work completed that day. 'Now, about the . . .'

'Not so fast, Ashley! Those glances you and your mother gave each other were quite expressive,' he interjected mockingly, fingers sliding into the back pockets of his pants. 'So what gives with those two, hmm? Has Jan suddenly decided to play hard to get?'

'No! Jan wouldn't dream of doing anything like that!'

'Then would you mind telling me just what is going on?' Dane pursued his line of questioning inexorably, his gaze satirical.

'Oh, for heaven's sake! You've missed your calling, you know that? You would have made a good inquisitor for the Spanish a few hundred years ago,' she glared at him in exasperation for his tenacity. 'Why should it bother you so much just because Mum and I happen to exchange a particular gesture or expression?'

'Because I don't like puzzles . . . and especially not when you're involved.'

'Meaning?'

'I thought you knew,' he taunted with a slow smile. 'I like to keep strict tabs on everything you do, honey. I'm still not quite sure I trust you.'

Hurt more than she liked to admit, but robbed of a retaliative anger by his tantalising smile, Ashley licked her lips and sent him a challenging look from beneath her lashes.

'Then, once again, aren't you taking an awful chance in allowing me a free hand with the furniture and fittings for the homestead? I might be tempted to purchase the most outlandish and hideous pieces I can find.'

Dane moved his head from side to side confidently. 'No, that's not your style. It's neither direct, nor personal enough for you, little one. You prefer to deliver all the crushing blows yourself,' he sardonically communicated the reasons for his certainty.

Crushing blows? That was a joke, grimaced Ashley dryly. She had never been able to even dent his vigilant guard, let alone crush it! And it was anything but a comfort to know he could forecast her reactions so accurately. There was no telling into which region such an ability might next lead him. She shuddered inwardly at the thought, but outwardly looked as uncaring as possible.

'You mean, I would if I could, don't you?' she quipped ruefully.

'Exactly my reason for making sure you never have the opportunity,' his teeth gleamed whitely against the darkness of his skin and his eyes glittered keenly within their absurdly long lashes. 'Which brings us right back to where we started. So why the exchange of looks in the kitchen?'

Ashley stared up at him in frustration and then spun away to stand by the newly installed sliding glass doors which led on to the verandah, jumping when another clap of thunder hammered at her ears.

'Because Jan's afraid of storms and she didn't want Leigh to find out,' she sighed.

'Is that all?'

There was no need to turn around for Ashley to know Dane was watching her incredulously. The signs were there in his voice, and she flung herself back to face him crossly.

'No, that is not all! Jan would rather keep to herself in her room when one of *these* takes place!' she spread a hand wide to disparage the raging elements outside.

'You don't consider Leigh capable of convincing her *he* should be the exception to that preference?' he questioned softly.

Ashley hunched away from the query moodily. 'I—I don't know,' she prevaricated—discomfitingly aware that every damned one of them was capable of charming the birds out of the trees if they set their mind to it. 'Jan was just worried he'd think her a baby for being so scared, I guess.'

'What? And miss out on a perfectly good excuse to put his arms round her? You underestimate him.' Dane's lips twitched in undeniable amusement.

'Perhaps.' Ashley flushed under his evocative gaze and turned her head aside so she didn't have to meet his eyes. 'But now—provided you feel sufficiently reassured that I had nothing more devious in mind when I looked at my mother in the kitchen, of course—do you think we could finally get around to discussing the homestead?' she asked with a defensively sweet sarcasm.

'Fire away.'

Both relieved and startled by his swift acquiescence, Ashley swallowed and launched into stammering speech. 'I—well, it's the carpets and the—the furniture mainly.' She paused and looked up at him appealingly, reverting to her original protest. 'Dane, I just can't choose all the furniture for your house!'

'I don't see why not. Just think of it as part of your job,' came the bland recommendation as he lightly shrugged off her objections. 'Now, what's the trouble with the carpets and furniture?'

With a sigh of defeat—it was patently obvious he had no intention of changing his mind—she eyed his sardonically. 'Well, for a start, where would you suggest I buy them? In Willow Bend?'

'Point taken! It looks as if you have a trip to Brisbane coming up, doesn't it?' he conceded wryly. 'Let's see ... now that the strip's completed Hal will be leaving for home next week to collect the plane, but once he returns he can fly you across to the coast whenever it suits. That okay?'

'I suppose so,' she shrugged tentatively, somewhat taken aback by the speed and manner in which he had disposed of the problem, and suddenly finding her long suppressed curiosity struggling to the surface so that she had to ask,

'When you buy a new property do you three always join together to do the work?'

'Usually,' he nodded. 'Most of the time we're kept busy with our own properties, so it becomes a good excuse for a family reunion.'

'But what about Brent? Doesn't he ever join in?'

'Not now that he and Leonie—that's his wife—have children. Although they'll be coming down here for the celebrations once the renovations are finished.'

Ashley's eyes rounded in surprise—that was the first she had heard of any forthcoming celebrations—but the discovery gave her the courage to seek a definite answer to a premise which, up until now, was still only conjecture. 'You're actually planning to live here for a while, then?' she probed diffidently.

'For the moment that's the general idea,' he drawled, although there was nothing indolent about his alert green gaze as it ranged over her reddening features. 'Were you hoping otherwise?'

'It matters little to me where you live,' Ashley was pushed into protecting herself mockingly. 'I only asked because everyone supposed you would be, but no one seemed able to say for sure.'

'Ted didn't tell you?'

'Ted?' she repeated with a frown. 'How long has he known?'

'Approximately ten years,' she was advised dryly. 'We've been corresponding ever since I left.'

'You've been . . .' Ashley couldn't believe her ears. 'You mean, he *knew* you were still interested in Kindyerra? That you were Jack Prescott's mysterious buyer?' Yet Ted had never once mentioned it to her! But now she knew why he had spoken so sharply to Nellie that night, and where the conviction for all those seemingly profound utterances had come from. Oh, she could scream for having been taken in so easily! 'And you had the hide to reckon I'd had my chances! Some chance with the pair of you working against me! How amusing it must have been for you to see me struggling to make ends meet when you knew damned well the whole thing was rigged from the start!' she blazed at him contemptuously, dragging open the sliding door and stepping out on to the verandah.

Dane's hand was there to impede the door being shut behind her and then he was grabbing hold of her arm and shaking her roughly. 'And where the hell do you think you're going in this, you little idiot?' He had to shout to make himself heard above the violent wind which had now blown up, as well as the almost continuous rolling of thunder.

'To see your fifth columnist, that's where! Not that it's any of your damned business!' Ashley shouted back furiously, her clenched hand lashing out towards the side of his head as she battled against his ensnaring grip.

Her wrist was captured and held with ridiculous ease before it could ever reach its objective and Dane's dark head lowered menacingly to disallow, 'Not in the mood you're in, you're not! You'd break his heart if you charged down there with that type of crazy accusation tripping off your tongue!'

'And what about my feelings?' she demanded breathlessly between her struggles. 'Neither of you cared about those while your unscrupulous little plan was in progress, did you?'

'For God's sake, Ashley, that's absurd!' He let go of one arm in order to rake a hand through his tousled hair, but the momentary easing of his hold was enough to have her wrenching completely free and racing along the verandah and down the steps without waiting for him to complete his ejaculated, 'There was no ...'

Nor did she stop her headlong flight into the choking haze of dust the wind was harrying when she heard him shout her name, although a brief look over her shoulder showed him to be determinedly giving chase. With a rapidly indrawn breath she urged her legs to a faster pace, for even above the roar of the storm she could hear his footfalls closing ominously, but she was still only just level with the machine shed when his hand descended on to the nape of her neck and she was unceremoniously propelled into its shadowy interior.

'Now stand still and bloody well listen to what you're told!' he shook her so savagely she wondered her teeth didn't come loose. 'There was no plan between Ted and me. We corresponded, that's all!'

Ashley impatiently brushed back the hair which had fallen across her forehead. 'And I wouldn't need to be very bright to guness what about,' she retorted bitterly. 'He writes and says how bad things are, and then you write back and suggest ways in which they can be made to deteriorate even further!'

'You little . . .!' The remainder of his denunciation was lost in a roll of thunder. 'If you were a man . . .'

'You'd hit me? Well, don't let the fact that I'm a female stop you. It didn't once before,' she dared to goad.

With a smothered curse, Dane swung away from her violently, the tension surrounding him almost palpable as he sought to exercise some control. 'God Almighty, you provoke a man into wanting to do just that sometimes, Ashley!' he lashed out harshly. 'No matter what I do or say, that's always there between us, and you can't resist returning to it like a moth fascinated by a flame!' His thumbs hooked into the belt about his lithe waist and in the light from the doorway she could see the wide shoulders move impassively beneath his bush shirt. 'Well, go and see Ted, if that's what you want. Maybe he'll be able to convince you where I can't.'

Timidly Ashley put out a hand towards the muscled back confronting her, and then withdrew it. She had never intended or wished to alienate him so completely, but having done so she wasn't certain which was the best course to follow in attempting to overcome it. Eventually, Dane made the decision for her.

'Get moving, Ashley!' he ordered implacably. 'There's nothing more we have to say to each other.'

Sighing helplessly, she obeyed, ducking past him and heading quickly for the doorway, then continuing on the path towards Ted and Nellie's cottage. With her head

downbent for protection against the flying dust she didn't
see the fracturing limb of an old jacaranda begin to sway
perilously, her only intimation of danger being the piercing
crack as it was finally torn free from the mighty trunk.

It was only natural that it should have been Dane's name
which sprang so automatically to her lips, Ashley told
herself later, but how he reached her in time to shelter her
close against the side of the shed with his own body she
never knew. Luckily only the fern-like leaves on the longest
bough managed to slap at them as the great mass slammed
resoundingly to the ground, but it was a sufficiently close
call to set Ashley's legs trembling weakly.

Dane lifted his head and shook it in disbelief. 'I'm
wondering which of us is the bigger fool,' his mouth
curved wryly. 'You, for coming out here ... or myself, for
following you.'

Pleasurably savouring the feel of his arms still pressing
her tightly to his powerful form, Ashley tilted her head
backwards to demur softly, 'I didn't ask you to foll . . .'

A hand laid gently but resolutely across her lips was an
effective silencer. 'How could I do anything else when I
knew that your intention was to denounce Ted? He was
never disloyal to you, honey, you should know that,' he
tried to impress on her quietly.

Discovering her lips to be softening traitorously, caress-
ingly, against the palm of his hand, Ashley drew her head
back swiftly. 'What did you write about, then?' she
prompted.

'Oh, Ted kept me informed of how things were going on
Kindyerra, of course. Why else do you thing those loans of
yours went through so effortlessly?' a distant sky-rending
flare showed his eyes shining with humour. 'But I certainly
didn't make any suggestions—one way or the other—as
to what should be done with the property.'

'Why make the loans available at all if you were so
anxious to get Kindyerra back again?' she puzzled. 'You
probably would have gained control years ago if you'd refused them.'

'Believe me, that's a question I've asked myself more

than once over the years,' he rubbed a rueful hand round the back of his neck as his chest rose and fell sharply on a deep sigh. 'You were such an aggravating little brat when I left that I've never been sure whether I was primarily motivated by a desire to give you enough rope to hang yourself, or whether, in accordance with Ted's recommendation of the time, it was to give you a chance to prove your capabilities after your father died.'

He was being nothing if not honest, she mused wryly. 'But fortunately for you, I obligingly hanged myself,' she grimaced.

'As long as you really believe that.' And in response to her enquiring frown, 'That it was you who did the hanging, and not Ted or I.'

Ashley dropped her gaze shamefacedly to the vicinity of his tanned throat and nodded. 'I'm sorry. I guess I shouldn't have been so ready to jump to the wrong conclusion.'

'It would seem we both suffer from the same complaint—neither of us completely trusts the other,' Dane generously eased away some of her embarrassment. Then, 'We'd better be getting back to the house before your mother starts to worry about your absence.'

Content with one arm securing her close to his side as they bent slightly into the wind, Ashley angled him a sideways glance from hesitant eyes, loath to shatter their temporary concord but unable to abstain from voicing the viewpoint which constantly trespassed in her mind.

'I still think you ought to let Della select her own furnishings,' sighing in relief for having found the courage to actually say what she meant.

Dane's reply was anything but what she had anticipated, however. Both brows lifted ironically as he exclaimed, 'I wasn't aware I was stopping her.'

'But the house . . .?' Ashley began in bewilderment, and then clamped her teeth together indomitably. Propriety be damned, she had gone too far to back off now! Pulling them both to a halt, she faced him with her hands on her slender waist and openly challenged, 'Are you, or are you not, going to marry Della Marchant?'

For the second time in as many minutes Dane's reaction was totally unexpected. He roared with laughter. 'Like hell I am!'

'But I thought . . .'

'That was who I was doing the homestead up for?' he smiled broadly and moved his head negatively. 'Uh-uh! You've got your wires crossed somewhere, honey.'

'Then why didn't you want her to see it before it was completed?' There were still some small fragments of doubt remaining.

'Because as you saw this afternoon Della has a habit of wanting to take control, so I considered it would save me the inconvenience and embarrassment of telling my former hostess to mind her own business if there was no opportunity for her to get in on the act before it was finalised.'

'Oh,' she breathed softly. That explained a lot of things. First and foremost, the reason why he hadn't asked Della to choose the fittings. As well as that, there was what she had privately considered to be his unloverlike attitude because she knew he had only infrequently seen Della since coming to stay at Kindyerra.

Although as they began walking again, instead of feeling elated at having disposed of their neighbour as a likely candidate for marriage, new problems crept into her mind. Then who was he going to all this trouble and expense for? Some girl he knew in Queensland where he had lived previously? She wondered what his reaction would be if she just came right out and asked him as she had with regard to Della. Somehow she doubted she would be as successful if she tried the same approach a second time— Dane's wasn't the temperament to meekly accept an excessive interest in his private life—and she wisely stilled the questions hovering on the end of her tongue. A long talk with Hal might prove just as informative, was her final shrewd decision.

CHAPTER NINE

THE storm exhausted itself during the evening and by next morning the sky had returned to its normal cloudless hue and the suffocating heat of the day before had diminished. Waiting until Dane and his brothers had departed after breakfast for an inspection of damage, Ashley wandered down the path to where Ted was occupied with the chain saw in lopping the fallen branches of the jacaranda into moveable lengths. There was no use in trying to make herself heard above its continuous drone, so she watched until he finished the cut he was making and then switched the motor off.

He was the first to speak. 'You wanted me for something, Ashley?'

'To ask you something really,' she half smiled as she seated herself on the thickest part of the branch. 'Why didn't you tell me you'd been writing to Dane all these years?'

Before answering Ted laid the saw on the ground and came to sit beside her, pulling his pipe from the pocket of his shirt, filling it methodically from the small tin he always carried with him, and finally putting a match to it. After a few igniting puffs he turned to look at her.

'You wouldn't have been pleased.'

She gave him a wry look from the corner of her eye. 'Since when did that worry you? You've never been backward in letting me know the unpleasant facts before.'

'That was business,' he smiled, unperturbed. 'But where Dane's concerned you've always let your emotions blind your reason, so I thought it best for you not to know.'

'Even though you knew his main objective has always been to redeem Kindyerra?' she bypassed the subtle rebuke and came straight to the point.

'What did that have to do with it?' He sounded genuinely

151

surprised. 'He was more than fair in his dealings with you.'

'I think I'm going to regret having started this conversation if you keep rapping me over the knuckles,' she grimaced ruefully, for in all truth she couldn't dispute his assertion because Dane had given them better terms and conditions in connection with his loans than they would probably have received elsewhere. 'But you might at least have given me a clue as to who was buying the place that night we decided to see Jack Prescott, instead of making all those supposedly prophetic remarks about the next owner caring and being good for the place.'

Ted's eyes glowed darkly with amusement. 'Somehow I just couldn't see you welcoming the knowledge,' he chuckled unrestrainedly, and Ashley eventually, grudgingly, joined in. Maybe in circumstances such as those ignorance was bliss!

'Okay, you old schemer, that's one to you,' she vouchsafed with a grin, plucking a long leaf from the branch and studiously drawing it between her fingers, her face gradually sobering. 'But I don't suppose Dane happened to—er —mention in any of those letters who he intended bringing to—um—live here, did he?' with a superficial nonchalance.

His teeth clenched on the stem of his pipe and his head moved unhelpfully. 'Not that I can remember.'

'No names at all?' she wrinkled her nose despondently.

'You know, if you hadn't already told me differently, I'd think you were showing an enormous amount of interest in someone else's affairs,' he commented artlessly.

'Oh, of course I'm not!' Ashley declaimed hastily, jumping to her feet and brushing the palms of her hands over the seat of her denims. 'It's a natural curiosity, that's all!' If she wasn't careful she would have him decidedly suspicious. 'Well, I suppose I'd better not hold you up for too long,' she smiled nervously. 'If you're going out later to help re-fence the woolshed yards I might go with you, though.'

'Right you are,' he nodded accommodatingly as he tapped

out his pipe and replaced it in his pocket. 'I'll give you a call when I'm ready to leave.'

She raised a hand and smiled in acknowledgment, watching while he held the cord of the saw and thrust the blade forward into operation and its resonance split the still morning air before heading back the way she had come.

Slipping into the office chair moments later Ashley pulled a sheaf of papers towards her and then sighed, leaning back in her seat and clasping her hands behind her head. Well, her attempt to question Ted had been pretty much of a fiasco! Not only had she failed to discover anything worthwhile, but after only one slightly ambivalent reply she had immediately panicked and beaten an inglorious retreat. It would have been far more convincing to have stayed and outfaced his provoking comment. By leaving in such a flustered hurry she had probably aroused his speculations rather than allayed them, and Ted was too perceptive to be seeing that type of response too often without guessing at the cause. She expelled her breath disconsolately and moved forward to pick up a pen. Oh, well, at least she had the trip out to the yards to look forward to. It would be good to do some work out in the open instead of being confined to the office all day.

Ashley had worked on solidly for quite a while before being interrupted by Bruce's, 'Hi! I thought you were planning on going out to the yards today.'

'I still am,' she looked up with a smile as he moved some of the boxes away so he could make use of the normal resting place. 'But I thought I'd get these done first and then go with Ted when he's finished disposing of the jacaranda.' Her head tilted and she sent him a teasing look. 'I must say you're looking very bright-eyed and bushy-tailed this morning, though. I suppose it's a relief to be rid of that plaster you've been carting around of late.'

'That's certainly a part of it—but only part.' He grinned to see her expression change to one of puzzlement.

'Okay, I'm intrigued,' she laughed. 'What's the rest of it?'

'W-e-ll,' the word was drawn out impressively. 'I had

quite a discussion with Dane before breakfast.'

'And?'

'You know the garage in town?' She nodded rapidly and he continued, 'Dane's volunteered to finance me in taking up the partnership I was offered.'

Knowing how much it meant to him, Ashley was as delighted as he was. 'Oh, Bruce, I'm so pleased for you. That's marvellous!' she exclaimed animatedly, eyes shining. 'Although I had no idea Dane would be interested in putting money into such a venture.'

He brushed a hand through his hair and admitted wryly, 'Neither had I, otherwise I doubt if I'd have spoken about it so freely with him.'

'Then perhaps it's just as well,' she laughed, and leant back in her chair to assert, 'It will make all the difference to you and Sheila, though.'

'That it will! I was never happy about asking her to marry me while the property was in such a bad way, but now . . .'

'It's all systems go, go, go!' she inserted with a chuckle.

'Something like that,' he smiled. 'I had already arranged to see her tonight, but now I have a doubly good reason for doing so.'

'You reckon we can expect to see an announcement in the paper shortly, then?'

'Never count your chickens before they're hatched,' was his mock-serious advice as he rose to his feet and moved towards the door. 'You never know, she just might refuse me.'

Ashley's rejoinder was a dry, 'I can imagine!' which had him grinning in reply and brought a carefree whistle to his lips as he jogged down the steps.

Feeling less like doing clerical work now than ever, Ashley tidied the papers lying on the desk and pushed back her chair. She would collect her hat from her room and help Ted to finish off if he wasn't ready yet. It was too nice a day to spend much of it indoors.

As it happened, she met Ted already on his way to tell her he was about to leave as she was walking down the

path, and with reciprocal smiles they turned as of one
accord for the garage. This time it was he who did the
driving, and as they passed the cottages Ashley looked
across at them with interest.

'They certainly look different these days too,' she commented thoughtfully, then with an enquiring look at the
man next to her, 'How does Nellie like the improvements,
Ted?'

His face broke into a broad grin. 'Pretty much, I reckon.
She can't stop talking about them.'

Ashley only wished she could have been the one to have
repaid them both in like measure for their help over the
years, but unfortunately there would never be any chance of
that happening now. In a few months she would be leaving
Kindyerra for good and ... She shied away from the
thought dejectedly and hurriedly began to talk about something else.

When they arrived at the yards the others were nowhere
to be seen and after assisting to unload the materials and
equipment they had brought with them in the ute, Ashley
wandered through the maze of pens, mentally deciding
which fences would need to be entirely renewed and which
ones only required marginal modification. At the end of the
tour she was pulling a disgruntled face and had lost count
of the numbers. It seemed that just about all of them were
in an extremely advanced state of disrepair!

'Here they come now,' Ted drew her attention to the
hazy red cloud which approached from the far corner of
the paddock, and from hand-shaded eyes Ashley watched the
truck which had been used to float the Carmichael horses
down to Billambang come rumbling towards them over the
hard-baked earth. Evidently someone else had come to
the same decision as she had, she thought ruefully, for the
vehicle was now piled high with solid wooden rails and
posts.

'Sorry we're late,' Dane apologised as he climbed down
out of the cabin. 'Though I'm pleased to report that there
doesn't seem to be any storm damage of note in the parts
we've covered so far.' He turned to look in the direction

from which they had come. 'A few old trees losing branches like the jacaranda, but that's about all.'

At this stage there seemed little for Ashley to do, so she waited until all they needed was assembled on the ground and it had been decided which of the yards were to be attended to first.

'What about me? What can I do?' she then asked as Dane passed by where she was standing beside the ute.

He indicated a tall belah beside the fence. 'You can sit in the shade. If I remember correctly, you do that quite well,' his mouth quirked teasingly. 'You can also shout encouragement from time to time, or else hand out the cold drinks.'

'Oh, very cute!' Ashley commended sarcastically. 'But now would you mind answering my question?'

Placing a hand on the top rail, Dane agilely cleared the fence in one smooth movement. 'I did answer it, honey,' he turned to retort from the other side. 'This is no work for you.'

'That's ridiculous—I've done it lots of times! And—and don't you dare make one of your sardonic remarks like, "Yeah, so I see",' she ordered hotly as she saw a certain expression crossing his face. 'Why can't I help?'

'Because this isn't what I pay you for.'

'You don't pay me to sit in the shade and hand out drinks either,' pertly.

His eyes flashed over her humorously. 'Don't remind me—I might be tempted to send you back to the homestead,' he threatened lazily.

The warning was only casually given but it was sufficient to forcibly bring home to her the fact that she wasn't free to work out on the property any more when she chose to, and momentarily she stared at him with suddenly tear-wet eyes before dropping her gaze and nodding mutely. It was even more difficult than she had realised it would be to reconcile herself to the idea that Dane was in sole charge of the property now and not herself.

Looking down on her bowed head, Dane softly smothered an exclamation. 'Oh, come on, then,' he urged with resigned forbearance. 'You can give Hal a hand.'

Ashley's head came up sharply to find his arm extended to help her over the rails. Needing no second bidding, she moved forward swiftly and, leaning across, Dane swung her effortlessly into his arms and deposited her on the ground beside him.

'I told you once before about looking at me like that, didn't I?' he cautioned wryly.

He had also kissed her on that occasion and, subconsciously, Ashley knew she was wishing he would do the same now. In an effort to dismiss the tormenting thought she swallowed hard and whispered, 'I'm sorry,' as she dragged her glance from his and concentrated on Hal's figure a couple of pens away.

'Just remember—I only said you could give him a hand. If I catch you attempting any of the heavy work, you're back to being a decoration. Right?'

'Right,' she assented quickly, without raising her head, and hurried to push through the gate which led into the next yard before he had a chance to change his mind.

As she clambered over the last fence and promptly went to work alongside him, Hal looked up and greeted her arrival with a grin. 'You must have done some hard talking,' he surmised with a wink. 'After Dane's remarks in the truck when he saw you here with Ted, I expected to see you relegated to the sidelines for the whole of the morning.'

'Oh, and what remarks might they have been?'

'Not for publication,' he revealed with a laugh and a shake of his head. 'Let's just say I don't think he was exactly enamoured with the situation.'

'Because he doesn't think I'm capable of helping?' Ashley flared, taking out her dissatisfaction on an old piece of wire by reefing it from the fence in one furious motion.

Again Hal shook his head. 'Because there's no need for you to do a station hand's work any more,' she was corrected implicitly before he went on to advise, 'That's what we're here for, little one,' in ironic tones.

'In other words ... I should remember that *he* owns

Kindyerra now, and I'm pushing myself where I'm not wanted?'

Hal couldn't have hidden his astonishment if he had tried. 'Good lord! No wonder you continually set Dane ticking like a time bomb if you twist his words that way,' he half laughed in disbelief. 'The idea was to relieve you of the hard work, not to disparage your intentions.'

Thoughtfully Ashley sank down on to her haunches and snapped a broken slab of fencing free at the bottom of a post. 'But I'd still much rather work out here, even if it is only mending fences,' she assured him earnestly.

'So I'd gathered,' he submitted dryly, breaking the rail off from its supporting post at the other end. 'Although, under the circumstances, that's not really the point, is it? The point is ... does Dane prefer it?'

'You mean, just because he's prejudiced against the female sex, I'm expected to—to ...' she faltered as a result of Hal's interjecting chuckle and ironically raised brows.

'I recommend you re-word your argument, blondie,' he smiled broadly. 'I can't ever remember a time when I would have said Dane was prejudiced *against* your sex!'

'No doubt!' she gibed rapidly to cover her own embarrassment in not choosing her words more carefully. 'But that wasn't what ...' She stopped and gazed up at him enquiringly. 'Is that honestly the type he goes for? The wildly helpless, faint at the sight of a mouse kind?' she elucidated in return for his own puzzled look.

'I wouldn't have said so,' he shrugged, prising a battered sheet of corrugated iron loose and tossing it on to the ever-growing pile of rubbish. 'But since we both have properties of our own these days I, naturally enough, don't always get to see who he's escorting around.'

Ashley resolutely pretended deep concentration with a stubborn nail. 'And his current girl-friend? I mean—I presume he does have one,' with just the right amount of indifference to convert her interest from personal to purely conversational. 'What's she like?'

'Lucia?' he exclaimed, the admiring tone causing Ashley

to spare him a covert glance from beneath her lashes. 'She's a doll! A real good sort!'

Depressed, and not a little chagrined by Hal's obvious approval, she found it difficult to keep her voice quietly affable for the next question. 'After a description like that I would have to assume it was serious. Is it?' she made herself laugh lightly, although the strain in doing so was tremendous.

Hal lifted his shoulders to emphasise his lack of knowledge. 'Who can say? If he is, he'll no doubt let us know in his own good time.'

Which wasn't a very satisfactory answer from Ashley's point of view because it meant that Hal knew little more than she did concerning Dane's future plans. However, he was a source of information regarding the absent Lucia and she intended to make full use of it.

Partially turning her back to him so it would appear she had lost interest in the subject, she continued with her work for some minutes before asking, as if the thought had only just occurred to her, 'This Lucia—has he known her for long?'

'Just on a year,' came the soft reply which had her stomach muscles contracting nervously and her face flushing even before she had wheeled around to receive Dane's taunting gaze and even more discomfiting, 'Anything else you'd like to know?'

As both Dane and Leigh had discarded their shirts some time back—an action Hal was now copying—Ashley also found herself confronted by a wide expanse of bare skin tanned the colour of polished mahogany, under which the hard muscles rippled vibrantly. A fact which did nothing to help restore her poise, and when combined with his baiting enquiry was quite sufficient to have her floundering in a turbulent sea of unruly emotions.

To make matters worse—if that was possible—Hal was apparently in a sportive mood, for he now gave her a sly nudge and suggested, 'While I'm getting the new rails for the fence, why don't you take him up on his offer? He's the right man to give you your answers.'

'Meaning?' Dane asked as soon as his brother was on his way.

'Oh—er—nothing really. You know what Hal's like,' Ashley laughed shakily, cursing Hal for putting her in such an invidious position, and in an attempt to distract Dane's attention queried innocently, 'Was there something you wanted to see me about?'

'Only to make certain you were keeping to our bargain,' he advised evenly, then leant across the railings which separated them to hook a forefinger into the open vee of her shirt and draw her unresistingly towards him. 'I'm the right person to give you which answers?' he prompted indolently.

His fleeting touch against the rounded swell of her breasts had Ashley's cheeks flaming an even deeper colour than they had been, and so shattered her thoughts that it was impossible for her to even think of the question let alone evade them. To give herself time to gather her wits she made a play of dragging her hat from her head and ruffling a hand through her golden hair before setting it back in place.

Licking dry lips, she shrugged uncaringly. 'Hal was just trying to put me on the spot. We were only talking generally, that's all.'

'About Lucia?' His expression was so sardonic it was obvious he didn't believe her, and she tried again— desperately.

'I—well—yes, her name did come into it,' she allowed uncomfortably.

'How?'

'How?' By repeating his question Ashley sought to gain a short breathing space. 'I—I'm not sure, actually. You know how these things happen,' she smiled weakly, darting a glance past him to see what was keeping Hal so long, and inwardly groaning as she discovered him to be talking to the others.

'No, I don't know in this instance—I wasn't here at the time,' Dane reminded her persistently, inscrutably. 'That's why I'm waiting for you to tell me.'

Ashley took a deep breath and ventured a conciliating, 'Does it matter?'

'Evidently it does to me,' he mocked, those glittering green eyes of his unbearably goading, 'or I wouldn't be asking, would I?'

If Ashley could have gauged what his reaction was likely to be it would have made her task a good deal more simple, but as her thought processes were annoyingly refusing to unite owing to their preoccupation with his dominant masculinity, utter confusion reigned and she had only her instincts to guide her.

'No—no, I suppose not,' she conceded finally, two deep furrows making an appearance between her finely marked brows. 'Well, we were—um—discussing something or the other . . . I can't remember just what.' She could, of course, but she wasn't about to give Dane a chance to expound his views on the equality of the sexes! 'And—and then I asked Hal if he knew what your present girl-friend was like,' she concluded breathlessly.

'Which, when added to the information regarding how long I've known her, tells you . . . what?'

It wasn't usual for Ashley to be so defensive and the disquieting knowledge that she was acting out of character fortunately gave her the impetus to return to the attack with a gibing, 'Don't worry, you don't have to spell it out, I'll say it for you. It tells me to mind my own damned business and stop prying!'

The angle of his head was a taunt in itself. 'Wrong again! Didn't I obligingly ask you if there was anything else you wanted to know?'

'Oh, sure! Although I would've said the question was sarcastic rather than obliging,' she retorted swiftly. 'But no, thanks, anyway! As I've already said, we were only talking generally. I'm really not all that interested in any of the loves of your life—old or new!' Which was probably the most brazen lie she had ever spoken in her life, as well as being the most necessary.

Dane's teeth showed startlingly white in an unanticipated laugh as he held her head between both his hands and drawled, 'Brat!' in lazy retaliation.

He was gone before Ashley could formulate a cutting reply—any reply, in fact—because it took some time for her senses to regain their equilibrium. His was the most mentally and physically disturbing personality she had ever known, and one which she was progressively finding more and more arduous to challenge, or disregard. If the truth be known, she mused ruefully, she wanted to do neither, and therein lay the cause for the majority of her problems!

Looking over the pens to where he stood lighting a cigarette and conversing with his brothers, Ashley surreptitiously watched the play of sunlight on his smoothly powerful back and shoulders, making it appear as though his flesh was a darkly glazed marble, and then with an aching sigh she turned away to pick up a pair of fencing pliers. If only the drought hadn't come then none of this would be happening! If only . . .

By lunchtime Ashley was glad to return to the homestead. By no means could she have called the morning a success, and only a desperate determination to prevent Dane from guessing at the havoc he could create within her had kept her out there so long. Working in such close proximity with him just wasn't comparable to the easy-going relationship she had shared with Ted on such activities.

'You look tired, love. Was it hot at the yards this morning?' her mother enquired sympathetically when Ashley wandered disconsolately into the kitchen prior to the meal.

Ashley shook her head but had to wait until a particularly vigorous bout of hammering in the lounge had ceased before shrugging, 'Only so-so,' in an indifferent voice as she leant back against one of the cupboards. 'We got a fair bit done, though.'

'Then I expect you'll all have worked up a good appetite for lunch,' Ruth smiled. 'It shouldn't be long now—I just have to cut the tomatoes.'

'No hurry,' Ashley counselled impassively. 'They're still talking to Ted down at the sheds.'

Ruth cast a worried look towards the wall clock. 'Oh, dear, do you think they'll be long?'

'I wouldn't have a clue.' Ashley helped herself to a piece of cheese and glanced at her mother curiously. 'Why? Have you something planned for this afternoon?'

To her astonishment her mother became quite nervous as she explained, 'Well, yes, I—I do really. In fact, I—I was going to ask you if you wouldn't mind seeing to tonight's meal for me.'

'Of course I don't mind,' Ashley smiled, forgetting her own worries with this new development and eyeing her parent more closely. 'But where are you off to? Just what is it that you have planned?'

Tomatoes began disappearing under Ruth's knife at a furious pace. 'Ramsay has invited me to—er—accompany him when he drives up to visit some friends of his at Sherbrooke after lunch.' Abruptly she raised her head to ask uneasily, 'You don't mind, do you, Ashley?'

'Good grief, no! Why should I?'

'Well, it did cross my mind that perhaps, with you having been so close to your father ...' She implicitly left the sentence unfinished.

Ashley moved her head emphatically. 'But he's been gone for seven years now, and I never was a fan for the belief that widows aren't entitled to any enjoyment in life whatsoever just because their husbands had the misfortune to die. Besides,' a teasing grin etched its way impishly across her face, 'it hasn't exactly gone unnoticed that Ramsay has been, how shall I put it?—very mindful of your presence?— for quite a while now.'

Ruth's happy expression showed her agreement, and relief. 'Yes, he is a very kind and considerate man, isn't he?'

As Ashley didn't really think her mother needed a verbal confirmation of this statement she pressed on with another question. 'Do Bruce and Jan know you're going out with him today?' she asked.

'Bruce does, but I'm afraid Jan was in rather a hurry this morning so I didn't have much time to talk to her.'

'Mmm, it looks as if I'm elected to do the honours, then,

seeing Bruce will probably have left for Sheila's before Jan arrives home. In the meantime, however,' she grinned, 'what time is Ramsay due to call for you?'

'At two, and I still have to dress yet,' her mother replied with another worried look towards the clock.

'Never fear, I'll have them up here in double quick time for you,' Ashley promised, the novelty of arranging matters so her mother could be ready to greet a date on time appealing to her sense of humour. 'I'll ring that old cow bell we've still got in the office. You know, the one you used to call us with when we were kids? That should get the message across,' she laughed, and straight away set about suiting her actions to her words.

And get the message across it did! The promptness with which they washed and presented themselves at the table gave Ashley cause to grin as she set out the last of the salad bowls and platters.

'Where's the fire?' quipped Hal as they all took their seats.

'No fire,' Ashley grinned back. 'Mum's going out at two o'clock and she wanted to make sure everyone had lunch before she left.'

Briefly silence reigned and then Ruth put in anxiously, 'You'll be able to manage dinner all right, won't you, Ashley?' and was rewarded by a look of fond exasperation from her offspring.

'Right as rain—and especially since I've decided we'll be having a barbecue.' Her gaze rested pointedly, roguishly, on the three men opposite her.

Leigh looked first at one and then the other brother on either side of him. 'In other words ... *we're* doing the cooking,' he translated wryly.

'You might be, old son, but you can count me out,' laughed Hal jubilantly. 'I won't be in to dinner either.'

'Oh!' Leigh winked across at Ashley before asking, 'And why not?'

'Well, you see, while I was in town the other day I happened to get talking to a very nice little brunette who works in the bank and I'm taking her out tonight,' was the complacent explanation.

Bruce and Ashley exchanged smiles and chorused, 'Maureen Humphries,' simultaneously.

Hal grimaced in mock disgust. 'I should have known you two would recognise almost everyone in town by description. So much for keeping anything a secret round here!'

The general banter didn't stop there, but Ashley's own thoughts headed off at a tangent. So who did that leave in the homestead for dinner? Only Jan and Leigh, Dane and herself. She let out her breath heavily. Now wasn't that going to be a cosy foursome!

With Bruce's help Ashley began moving all the files and equipment from the old office into the new during the afternoon. This was the only part of the extensions to be completely finished so far and she found the experience thoroughly enjoyable in arranging the furniture which Hal and Leigh had brought round after lunch, and seeing that everything was neatly and compactly put away. Everything, that was, except her riding cups and trophies which she left packed in their cardboard carton. They could adorn her bedroom for the time being now that the property was sold.

At last she stood back and surveyed their handiwork judiciously. 'Well, what do you think of it?'

'Looks okay to me,' Bruce smiled. 'It leaves the other one for dead, doesn't it?'

'Sort of,' she agreed laconically, eyes twinkling. 'But now, if you want to go and get ready, I can dispose of all these,' indicating the discarded boxes and cartons piled up outside the doorway.

'Thanks, Ash.' He was already halfway to the door. 'If I don't get in the bathroom soon, I can see Hal beating me to it.'

'That's for sure,' she laughed after him, and then on an affectionate note, 'If I don't see you again before you leave ... good luck!'

Bruce raised one finger to his temple, grinned, and was gone.

Ashley had only just finished stacking the containers ready for burning when Hal returned from the yards early and walked back to the homestead with her.

'Bruce ready yet?' he asked.

'Probably. He left to have his shower a while ago.'

'I thought I might as well drop him off when I go—save him using the old rattletrap there,' he nodded back in the direction of the ute. 'I have to pass the Garretts' place on my way to and from town in any case.'

'Sounds fine to me,' she shrugged lightly. 'You'd better check with him.'

Apparently it was quite acceptable to her brother too, for a short time later they both came out to the kitchen to let her know they were leaving, with Hal unable to forbear adding a parting, 'Make sure you behave yourself while we're gone.'

'Oh, funny—very funny,' Ashley wrinkled her nose at him facetiously. 'You'd do better to reserve that little piece of advice for yourself. You do know that Maureen has five brothers and that three of them just happen to be in the police force, don't you?' with undisguised relish in the telling.

'I didn't—but I'll keep it in mind,' he returned irrepressibly, but with such a winning smile that Ashley felt almost sorry for her one-time school friend. Hal, like his brothers, was too damned attractive for any girl's peace of mind!

With their departure Ashley took the opportunity to make use of the bathroom herself and change into a coral knitted tube top which left her shoulders bare, and a pleated skirt of sand-coloured rayon, so that she could have most of the food ready to be taken out to the barbecue before the others arrived home. And it was just as well she had, she decided wryly, otherwise she would still have been in her old denims and shirt when Dane and Leigh returned to the homestead, for after breezing through the kitchen with only a rushed greeting Janelle had occupied the room up until a few minutes before they put in their appearance. While the two men were changing she came out to the kitchen to lend a hand, her happy expression turning to one of enquiry.

'Where's Mum?' eyes widening at the unexpected absence.

Ashley looked up from the long bread roll she had been slicing to smile, 'Ramsay Marchant invited her to go up to Sherbrooke with him to visit some friends. I don't expect she'll be back until late.'

'Ah-hah! So I was right!' Janelle seemed extremely pleased with something and recounted for her sister's benefit, 'I remarked to Leigh at the party that I thought Ramsay was showing Mum a considerable amount of very special attention.' Her eyes held Ashley's intently. 'Do you think she reciprocates his feelings?'

'I wouldn't like to commit myself fully on that one,' came the animated answer. 'Though I don't think I would be going too far if I said that, at the moment, she appears to have a definite lean in that direction.'

'She'd like living on Billambang,' Janelle stated categorically. 'She always did prefer station life and I think that's one of the reasons why she was so keen for you to make a go of this place—because she didn't really want to move into town either.'

Ashley conceded the assumption with a nod. 'I'll go along with you on your latter idea, but I don't know about the other. How could anyone enjoy living there with Della?'

'But Della won't be there much longer! Didn't you know? She's going into business with some friends of hers in Sydney. A boutique, or something like that, I believe.'

An occupation which should suit Della's not inconsiderable talents very well, Ashley allowed, and grinned ruefully. 'I had heard some mention of her moving, but actually . . .' she hesitated and then continued resolutely, 'I was under the impression until last night that she was marrying Dane and coming here to live.'

'Oh, Ashley, how could you even think of such a thing?' Janelle burst into peals of incredulous laughter. 'He's much too nice to wish that on him. Anyway,' she lowered her voice confidentially, 'from what Leigh's been telling me, I gather Dane's sights are well and truly turned in a very different direction.'

A corroborating statement Ashley had been dreading to hear. 'Yes, I discovered that for myself this morning too. It's a Lucia somebody or the other,' she disclosed flatly.

'So that's her name! Leigh either couldn't—or wouldn't —tell me that little morsel.'

'Well, Hal wasn't so reluctant. According to him she's quite something!' Ashley only just managed to stop herself from grimacing in time.

'That doesn't surprise me,' Janelle owned dryly. 'After all, when you've got the looks and personality he has, I should imagine you can take your pick of . . .'

'Watch it!'

Ashley's whispered warning had Janelle sending a stealthy glance over her shoulder, then turning back again with a suppressed grin as Dane and Leigh entered the room together, and querying, 'Would you like me to get the plates out for you now?' in such wide-eyed innocence that it was all Ashley could do to reply without revealing their rapid dissimulation by laughing.

CHAPTER TEN

FORTUNATELY the barbecue wasn't quite the harrowing experience Ashley had half expected it to be, although she had to admit that this was due to the other three's efforts to maintain a light friendly atmosphere rather than her own, because the more amiable Dane was, the harder she found it to respond naturally. At least when they were arguing she could stop acting a part and permit her true emotions to show instead of camouflaging them as she was forced to do the rest of the time.

The darkness outside was complete, apart from the dimmed garden lights, before the last of the utensils and the remaining edibles had been returned to the kitchen and their various niches. Coffee was quickly brewed, but when Janelle and Leigh took theirs into the lounge, Ashley lingered on in the kitchen hoping that Dane would follow them and thus give her the opportunity to seek the privacy of her bedroom without openly appearing to be avoiding them. But Dane showed no signs of wanting to leave, however, as he calmly put a flame to the end of his cigarette and then swung a chair round in one hand to straddle it on the opposite side of the table. With a barely concealed sigh Ashley pulled out a chair on her side and sank down on to it resignedly.

'Have you thought that if your mother's friendship with Ramsay should proceed to its natural conclusion we could find ourselves neighbours in the not too distant future?' was the lazy observation as his eyes flickered over her slowly.

In actual fact that same unsettling realisation *had* been in the forefront of her mind all afternoon, and it hadn't taken much contemplation on her part to know that it would be a situation she couldn't possibly endure. Now one shoulder was raised negligently.

'I doubt it,' she contradicted sharply.

'You don't think either of them are that serious?'

'I wasn't referring to Mum, or Ramsay. I just meant that I doubted I would live with them.'

'Why not?' he probed with a frown.

'Because *if* they did marry, then I think they're entitled to some time alone together and—and now that you've kindly relieved me of all my responsibilities,' with a provoking smile, 'there's nothing to stop me applying for station work elsewhere.'

'Where . . . elsewhere?'

Ashley eyed him mockingly over the rim of her cup and retorted flippantly, 'I'll tell you that when I've decided.'

'I only asked because I thought I might have been able to help,' he countered evenly, sending smoke ceilingwards. 'We have quite a number of connections throughout the eastern States.'

'Maybe, but I would still prefer to get my own job without any pressure being brought to bear, thanks all the same!' she gibed.

'I wasn't intending to use pressure. It was a suggestion to perhaps make things a little easier for you, that's all.'

The idea of being beholden to him appalled her. 'I can't recall saying I wanted them made easier,' she challenged, her arching brows a study in brashness. 'You see, as much as this may come as a shock, I don't happen to consider I *need* your help!'

Dane folded his arms along the back of his chair and advised wryly, 'But one of these days you're sure as hell going to need someone's, honey!'

'Oh, and why's that?' confidently.

'Because I can see the time coming very soon now when I finally put an end to your provoking little manoeuvres in one of two ways, and right at the moment I'm not certain you'd find either of them desirable!' he drawled.

Ashley's cup clattered noisily against its saucer as it was rapidly replaced. Suddenly she wasn't feeling quite so sure of herself any longer and her eyes searched his warily. Why his candid acknowledgment of her antagonism should have shaken her so much she couldn't have said—after all, he had implied the same on previous occasions—but, conversely, she *did* know she wouldn't be asking for any explanations. Something somewhere deep inside her was warning that this was not the time to press her luck!

But it did provide an opportunity to solve her most immediate problem. 'In that case, you won't object if I relieve you of my company,' preparing to rise to her feet.

'Not just yet,' he vetoed her escape with an imperative hand indicating she should stay where she was. 'I wanted a word with you regarding the office.'

'You don't like the way I've arranged it?'

Dane dismissed that theory with a shake of his head. 'You've forgotten the cups.'

'Cups?' At first she didn't follow him. 'Oh, you mean my cups. I didn't forget them, I put them away in my room.'

'Why?'

'I would have thought that was obvious,' she retorted, then prudently moderated her tone to a less taunting one. 'You're the owner of Kindyerra now, and they don't belong in there any more.'

'I'm the best judge of that,' was the autocratic answer which had her gritting her teeth in an endeavour to stay calm. 'The room looks too stark without some form of decoration.'

'So I'll buy you a couple of pictures to hang on the walls when I'm in Brisbane,' she quipped, and promptly started chewing unsteadily at her lip on receiving his lazy look of warning. 'Or—or ... I'm sure you must have some of your own to replace them,' with only a faint suggestion of sarcasm evident.

'But *I* see no reason to replace them,' she was advised aggravatingly as he rose lithely to his own feet this time. 'So how about you put them back again, hmm?'

'Okay,' Ashley sighed in defeat. 'When I get the time.'

'Now!' Dane stipulated inflexibly, softly dangerous.

'For heaven's sake!' she couldn't help giving voice to the exclamation. 'Why does it have to be right at this minute?'

'Because I wouldn't put it past you to—conveniently—forget.'

The thought had occurred to her too and she dropped her gaze guiltily, annoyed to know the colour of her cheeks was blatantly proving to him that his assumption had been correct.

'You're sure you wouldn't like to accompany me while I collect them?' she goaded caustically in an attempt to gain at least some of the initiative.

A smile shaped his mouth as if she had stated her intent aloud. 'No, I'll wait for you in the office. Just make certain you don't happen to mislay any of them on your way, that's all!' he cautioned.

This time Ashley had to admit that he was one step ahead. As yet, that idea hadn't occurred to her! But presently, when she retrieved the carton containing the trophies from her room, she was glad Dane had refused her mocking invitation to keep her under surveillance because she strongly doubted she would ever again have been capable of entering the room without recalling his magnetic and overwhelming presence had he once been there.

As promised, he was already in the office when she returned, leisurely reclining in the chair behind the desk, arms folded across his chest.

'Is there anywhere in particular you wanted them to go?' Ashley enquired sweetly as she deposited the box on the desk.

Dane waved an arm towards the bookshelves which ran the width of the room beneath the windows. 'I think that's the most obvious place,' he returned blandly, and with so much self-assurance that Ashley could have hit him, because she was feeling anything but confident or controlled.

She swung to face him a few minutes later after she had summarily done as he bid. 'There! Does that satisfy you?' her eyes widened baitingly.

His lips twitched in recognition of her evident resentment, but he said nothing, merely moving out of the chair and coming to stand beside her. Bending, he inspected the trophies more closely, in much the same manner as he had once before.

'I noticed that last time,' he smiled eventually and straightened. 'What happened to the year between those two?' pointing out the relevant show-jumping awards which, except for the year he was referring to, were part of a consecutive set of five. 'Didn't you even make runner-up?'

Ashley sucked in her breath swiftly and shook her head. 'No, I had to withdraw from the competition.'

'Horse trouble?'

'No!' she glared at him furiously, then, 'You do know just which year that was, don't you?'

'Mmm, I know,' he acknowledged laconically. The year circumstances had impelled him to resign from Kindyerra was indelibly imprinted in his memory too. 'So . . .?'

'The final rounds were held the day after you—you gave me a hiding,' she advised sarcastically, her breathing heavy. 'And I've already told you I—I could hardly sit or stand for the week after that!' came the concluding accusation.

Ashley had expected him to be amused by the discovery that his form of chastisement had been the cause of her withdrawal, but instead he sighed and ran a hand through his hair, somewhat wearily it seemed to her.

'Which is just one more good excuse to add another black mark against my name as far as you're concerned, isn't it, honey?' he deduced sardonically.

Up until his return that had definitely been the case, but ever since the night of the Marchants' party they seemed to have been receding further and further into the distance of her consciousness, only to be resurrected at those moments when she felt most vulnerable. As now, for instance? she mocked herself dolefully.

'Well, not even you could have supposed your actions likely to inspire hero-worship,' she pointed out, moving uncomfortably from one foot to the other. 'I mean, you *were* pretty lousy that day!'

One eyebrow peaked siginificantly. 'I wonder why?'

'All right, I'll grant you I wasn't the most endearing kid

around!' she vouchsafed, holding his tormenting gaze valiantly while her fingers curled helplessly at her sides. 'But I still say it wasn't altogether my fault.'

'No, your father can take a lot of the credit,' he nodded expressively.

'I was meaning *you*!' she insisted.

Some subtle change overtook his expression and Ashley was already licking at suddenly dry lips when he drawled softly, 'Are you challenging me to that showdown I spoke of earlier?'

'H-hardly!' she stuttered, and actually took a step backwards in her desire to retreat from the stand she had unconsciously been making. 'That would be rather stupid of me, wouldn't it? Especially when you've already warned me I—I wouldn't like the consequences.' A statement she didn't doubt in the slightest.

A finger trailed excitingly across the soft skin of her cheek and down the side of her neck, making her shiver with uncontrollable awareness.

'All that submissiveness,' he marvelled, a thread of amusement apparent in the depths of his pleasant voice. 'When in reality we both know you'd love nothing better than to see me hanged, drawn, and quartered!'

Ashley ventured a tentative glance from the cover of her lashes. 'You've got me all wrong,' she began innocently, but when his eyes had narrowed doubtfully, disclosed mockingly, 'I'm not that greedy—hanging will do!'

For one elated, light-headed moment, Ashley thought he meant to draw her unceremoniously into his arms. Then a muscle moved jerkily at the side of his jaw as if under a rigid discipline and he gave her a rueful smile instead.

'I'm not surprised you had Ralph losing his cool.'

'I like that!' she exploded indignantly, her hands coming up to rest aggressively on her hips. 'Next, I suppose you'll be telling me I invited him into the office for just that purpose!'

'Uh-uh!' he squashed the suggestion negligently—much to Ashley's relief. 'Believe me, if I had thought that, you wouldn't have received any help from me in extricating yourself.'

That just didn't fit in with what she knew of his character, somehow. 'Wouldn't you really have done anything to help?' Her blonde head tipped to one side quizzically.

'Maybe—maybe not,' Dane shrugged lightly, wryly, and then enquired, 'You coming?' over one shoulder as he made for the door.

Ashley nodded and followed thoughtfully. It wasn't like Dane to cut short a conversation as he had just done, and as she sought a reason for it she failed to come up with one she found satisfactory. It was almost as if he had suddenly tired of, or was anxious to be rid of, her company—an agonising thought which was to keep her restlessly awake long after she had retired to bed that night.

In the end it was Dane himself and not Hal who flew back to Queensland by charter in order to collect his plane, and during the time he was away Ashley was constantly plagued by mental images of the unknown Lucia clasped in his arms and being thoroughly kissed. It was the most miserable period of her life, and even though she kept telling herself that it was something she was going to have to learn to live with in the future, it didn't bring any respite from the aching void which seemed such a permanent part of her anatomy these days.

There wasn't even much of a chance to enjoy his return either, because forty-eight hours later Hal flew her to Brisbane for her shopping expedition. Under other conditions it could have been a trip to put her on cloud nine, but as it was her heart really wasn't in it and she went through the motions of selecting and discarding mechanically. Oh, she did her best—her pride saw to that—but there was no enjoyment to be experienced from each purchase at the end of the day, and the only thing she looked forward to was tumbling into bed at night for a few hours' blessed forgetfulness.

Hal was a godsend because he was unfailingly cheerful,

and thus prevented her spirits from dropping lower than they already were, and because he took care of so many things for her—taxi hire, freight arrangements, the location of the necessary stores and warehouses, even helping with the choice of drapes when Ashley was undecided.

A couple of times they went out in the evening—once to a nightclub and once to the theatre—but mostly they made use of the hotel's lounge and by way of the television kept a close watch on the hopeful rain clouds which were beginning to amass over the far north-west of the continent.

Much to Ashley's surprise, Dane had put through a telephone call every night, and although her heart would beat violently at the sound of his voice, her answers to any of his queries were so stilted that she usually made a point of handing the receiver to Hal as quickly as possible if he happened to be in her suite at the time.

After the fourth such call she had remarked mockingly, 'I get the feeling he doesn't trust me with this after all!' but as Hal's reply had been an oblique, 'There certainly seems to be something bugging him,' she had let the matter drop because she was finding that, in one way or another, seeking answers where Dane was concerned usually proved to be an extremely painful process.

They arrived back at Kindyerra to find the place a hive of excited anticipation. Not only was Bruce now planning a marriage—Sheila had given him a definite affirmative in that regard—but Janelle and Leigh were intending to celebrate their engagement very shortly, and on top of all this —overshadowing it, in fact—there was the vague promise of at least *some* rain because the low which had been centred in the west was now moving slowly eastwards, pouring forth the waters of deliverance as it went.

'Let's just hope it doesn't rain itself out before it gets this far,' commented Hal ruefully at dinner that night—a thought which had crossed all their minds more than once—and which now had them replying with varying degrees of optimism.

During the next few days the phone was in almost constant use as friends and acquaintances from further west

rang to pass on joyous tidings and information concerning
the torrential downpours they were receiving with open
arms, but it was to be another two days before those properties situated around Willow Bend could actually begin
to believe that, after all, their dreams might become a
reality.

The initial promising omen came at break of day. The
sky was lightly overcast, the sun throwing only a subdued
light for once, and a teasing sprinkle of rain fell to the
ground to lose itself immediately within the dust. But to
everyone's dismay, by breakfast the cloud cover began to
disperse into wispy trails of white against a background of
ever-brightening blue, and it quickly became a matter of
severely controlling rising hopes in case nature had per-
versely decided to either withhold her benevolence, or
deliver it elsewhere.

By mid-afternoon the prospects of Kindyerra receiving a
good fall had diminished acutely as messages received from
properties to the south of them indicated which areas had
been the fortunate ones, and it was only due to habit that
before resuming her work after one of these calls Ashley
glanced listlessly westwards.

The sight which met her eyes was unbelievable and, her
gaze widening, she leapt from her seat and raced out on
to the verandah for a clearer view. It couldn't be! her
mind argued incredulously, but her eyes kept telling her it
was. A second front was marching inexorably over the
horizon, so low that it appeared to only just clear the
distant trees, and so dark that it seemed like some menac-
ing purple-black bruise as it spread across the firmament
and contemptuously blotted out the fiery orb of the sun.
There was no doubt it was bringing rain—Ashley could
already see it falling in a heavy grey curtain as the clouds
rolled closer—and with a barely controlled shout of delight
she bounded down the steps and out into the open to await
its arrival.

The first drops came tentatively, digging deep craters
into the filmy top layer of earth, and then more frequently
to merge each separate depression into a smooth wet whole

until it was finally cascading down from the heavy mass overhead like a vertical river. In a matter of minutes she was drenched—her hair turning several shades darker as it became plastered to her head, her clothes clinging to her soddenly—but she couldn't have cared less! At last the drought had broken, and she was too busy enjoying the indescribable emotion such a time brings to worry about the triviality of getting wet.

'Ashley! Are you going to stand out there for the rest of the afternoon?' called Ruth Beaumont in an indulgent voice from the verandah. She could remember doing exactly the same thing once when she was young after a succession of particularly dry seasons had finally come to an end.

Angling her head away from the heavens, Ashley opened her eyes, looked across at her mother and grinned, 'No, I'm going to take Amarina and have a look at the dam and the tanks. If it continues to come down this heavily it won't take long for them to start holding water again.'

'Don't you think you ought to change and put on a coat or something before you go?' wryly.

'You could be right,' came the laughing reply as Ashley ducked back on to the verandah and stood looking down at herself ruefully—but unconcernedly. 'I do look somewhat bedraggled, don't I?'

'You do,' Ruth nodded so laconically that they both laughed.

A change of clothing was quickly accomplished and with the protection of a hat and a waterproof jacket, Ashley was soon trotting Amarina out of the yard and heading for the dam. This, of course, was one of the most important reservoirs on the property because it spanned a natural watercourse and a careful check had to be kept of its level so that, when necessary, the small sluice gate could be opened to enable any excess water to continue on downstream instead of eroding the built-up earth banks if it overflowed.

As she had expected, the bed of the creek between the dam and the next natural waterhole was still empty, but the downpour so far had been heavy enough to provide a shallow depth within the cavity of the dam itself and she swung to the ground and ran forward eagerly in order to inspect it more closely. Too late did she remember that she had left the reins looped across the little mare's neck instead of hanging in front to keep her standing, and worse still, after so long it had completely slipped her mind that Amarina had been a definite misnomer on her behalf, because if there was one thing her mount objected to working in, it was the *rain*!

At the first sound of a disgruntled snort behind her Ashley whirled swiftly with the mare's name on her lips— the recollections returning now—but with a graceful toss of her proud little head Amarina began heading for home, and none of Ashley's whistles or shouts could persuade her to alter course.

'You wait till I get back, you—you spoilt little mule!' she cried as the black form disappeared from sight amid the descending grey, then she laughed at herself ruefully.

It was her own fault and it wasn't as if it was the first time she had been forced to walk home from here—at least she should be thankful that on this occasion she had something on her feet! But before she started doing just that, Ashley decided she might as well take a closer look at the water in the dam. After all, that was the reason she had originally ridden all the way out here.

Standing at the edge, she removed her riding boots and socks and paddled out into the centre without bothering to turn up the legs of her jeans because they were soaking from the knees down anyway. To her delight it was already deep enough to lap warmly about her ankles and from the look of the clouds above there was still plenty more to come.

Suddenly the even tenor of the rain was disturbed by the louder sound of the vehicle engine and, thanking her lucky stars for its timely arrival, Ashley waded out of the water and raced up the bank, so whoever it was shouldn't miss seeing her. Through the rain it was difficult to tell who was driving and it wasn't until the ute had pulled to a halt beside her and the window wound down that she saw it was Dane.

'If it's not a silly question, would you mind telling me what on earth you thought you were doing in the middle of the dam?' His brows arched expressively.

This afternoon Ashley was too happy at seeing the drought broken to let anything like mockery dampen her spirits. 'I was testing the depth, naturally,' she returned earnestly. 'It's the best way of checking at that level.'

Dane's eyes went past her to the dam. 'At *that* level I wouldn't have said it rated checking at all,' he retorted.

'Oh, don't be such a killjoy!' she grinned. 'Aren't you pleased it's come at last? Just think,' her blue eyes twinkled disarmingly, 'those little green shoots which will start showing in a day or so will be all yours!'

'A fascinating thought,' he agreed wryly, 'and if I had my doubts before you've just laid them all to rest ... I now know you're a nut!'

'Because I'm happy to see the rain?'

'No, because you apparently prefer to stand in it to do your talking. For God's sake, why not get in and then I can wind this window up again,' he suddenly smiled.

The temptation was too great and she tilted her head slightly so that the water lodging on the brim of her hat splashed on to his shoulder and ran down his bare forearm. 'See? It doesn't hurt at all,' she sparkled incorrigibly.

To her surprise he merely shrugged casually, 'Okay, if you don't want a lift back to the homestead,' and began raising the window between them.

Before the action could be completed, however, Ashley had skidded around the front of the vehicle and clambered hastily into the seat beside him. Shrugging out of her jacket and laying it together with her hat on the shelf behind the seat she gave him a reproachful glance.

'You'd just love the chance to make me walk all that way again, wouldn't you?'

His lips moved humorously. 'It would serve you right for losing your mount like a beginner,' he lectured lazily, turning the ignition key and reversing away from the dam.

'Did you see her?' Ashley smiled and leant her head back against the seat. 'It wouldn't have been so bad except I'd forgotten she's always disliked bad weather.' Her eyes slanted sideways to gaze at him curiously. 'Have you got a thing about it too?' she quizzed.

'What makes you say that?'

'Well, I would have expected you to be overjoyed by all this,' she waved a hand towards the rain the wipers were having trouble clearing from the windscreen. 'Instead you're carrying on like some old grouch who's just lost his last dollar.'

Ashley guessed she must have touched a nerve somewhere because the ute slammed to a halt and Dane half turned in his seat to appraise her coolly.

'There are other ways of showing one's pleasure without resorting to childish antics like wading in the dam fully clothed,' he disparaged sarcastically.

'Quite possibly ... if you've only had to wait a few months for a drought to break!' she flared, sitting bolt upright now. 'But I haven't! I've been waiting for three long years—three damned long years—for this moment, and I'm not going to let you spoil it for me. You know something ...? This will probably give you a good laugh, but I was even feeling pleased for *your* sake that it rained!' Tears burnt at the back of her eyes and she blinked them away furiously. 'Oh, damn you, Dane Carmichael, I'd rather walk and enjoy the feel of the rain than sit here and suffer your petty sermonising!' She flung herself towards the door and grabbed at the handle.

'Come back here and stop being such a little idiot!'

A hand gripped her upper arm, dragging her bodily into the middle of the seat, and she hit out at him wildly, her breathing ragged. 'Yes, that's me! The brat ... the nut ... the idiot! And anything else uncomplimentary you can think of!' she choked resentfully, still struggling futilely against the restraining hands which had hold of both her arms now. 'Heaven help me, I must have been out of my tiny mind to let myself fa-ll ...'

Pearly white teeth snapped together almost audibly. Dear God, what was she saying? Finally she stopped straining against his grasp and sat deathly still, her head bent, her eyes closed. Hoping against hope he didn't realise the full import of those carelessly uttered words.

'Why stop there?' came the softly drawled prompting from somewhere above her head which sent all her hopes crashing in despair. 'It seems to me you'd only just reached the intriguing part.'

'Oh, go to hell!' Ashley tried to pull away from him bitterly. 'Making fun of me really turns you on, doesn't it?'

Dane released one of her arms in order to slide his fingers within her blonde hair and force her gaze up to his. 'No, this is what turns me on,' he contradicted huskily, drawing her relentlessly nearer to his warm length, and possessively covering her unconsciously waiting lips with his own.

All thought of resistance faded swiftly beneath his demanding kisses and Ashley surrendered willingly and un-inhibitedly, feeling the blood coursing feverishly within her body in time with the rapid pounding of her heart as she curled slender arms about his neck, her mind reeling as his hands swept her smooth-skinned back in a long caress beneath her freed shirt. She was trapped in a maelstrom of sensuous emotion she had never known before, and it wasn't until his mouth relinquished hers to sear a trail of fiery desire from her arching throat to the swelling curve of the pulsating breast cupped in his hand that her brain began to function again and she pushed herself frantically out of his embrace.

'Well, th-that's great, isn't it? F-for you!' Suddenly she became aware that her shirt was hanging open and affording him a view of a generous amount of inviting flesh and she refastened it hastily, her eyes dropping before his in embarrassment. 'But, for your information, it doesn't happen to do anything for me to—to . . .'

It was impossible to continue while his brows were sloping upwards with such lazy mockery and his mouth was fashioned in such a taunting expression, and she stared back at him in confusion, her cheeks flaming, her voice stilled.

'Then we shall have to see it does do something for you, won't we, honey?' Dane drawled, his very lethargy catching her unprepared for the agile movement which imprisoned her helplessly within his arms again.

'No!' Ashley immediately battled desperately to escape, knowing she would never be able to put a brake on her aroused emotions a second time, even if she wanted to—which was doubtful. 'You didn't let me finish! I—I . . .'

His lips brushed across hers only lightly, to her surprise —and disappointment, she suspected ruefully—but effectively interrupting her attempted explanation for all that.

'You *are* finished, honey,' he murmured cryptically. 'You just haven't realised it yet.'

Ashley's wary eyes sought his with a frown. 'I don't think I know what you mean.'

'I mean . . . my pretty, provoking little brat,' he smiled tantalisingly down at her, 'that unless you agree to marry me very shortly, I can see myself rapidly losing what little control is left to me and making love to you, thoroughly, before this day is out!'

The arms which had been holding her a firm captive loosened a little and Ashley used the opportunity to slide her hands between them and up to his head, drawing it closer to her softly parted lips as she vowed fervently, 'Oh, Dane, of course I'll marry you—tomorrow if it's possible! You know I love you, don't you?' and proved it by setting her mouth to his in a willing demonstration of the depth of her feelings.

'Dear God! Not half as much as I love you,' Dane groaned vehemently some long electrifying minutes later, smoothing her still damp hair back from her forehead. 'Why did you have to wait until it slipped out accidentally before giving me some indication of your feelings?'

Ashley dimpled piquantly. 'Why didn't you give me a sign as to how you felt?' she countered.

'I did,' he laughed, a richly deep sound. 'I told you at the Marchants' party that I loved you . . . remember?'

'That's not counted! You didn't mean it seriously,' she pouted.

'Maybe not when I thought it,' he conceded wryly, his expression evocative. 'But immediately I said the words aloud, I knew I meant them.'

'And I was wishing you had,' she sighed, then pulled her head back from where it was nestled against his shoulder to condemn, 'Though goodness knows why I should have done. You were a brute to me that night!'

'You asked for it. Your flag-waving independence was like a red rag to a bull where I was concerned,' he grinned impenitently at her indignant features. 'Besides, to my mind Hal was behaving far too proprietorially towards you and, what's more, you appeared to be enjoying it!'

'You were jealous!' she gasped in astonishment.

'More than likely,' he owned ruefully.

'Oh, Dane!' Her eyes slanted upwards regretfully for all the wasted time and arguments, and then something caught her attention and she swivelled round on the seat so she could inspect it properly. 'Is that what I did?' she bit at her lips contritely as she traced a finger down an inch-long thin white groove she could see at the side of his neck.

'Uh-uh,' was the succinct acknowledgment. 'You always were a handful.'

'I am sorry,' Ashley laid her mouth against the mark softly and then slid back into her former position tucked close beneath his arm, her head on his shoulder, and one hand resting on his broad chest. 'Apart from having that to remind you, did you ever think about me during all those years you were away?' She flicked him a shy smile.

Dane's hold tightened fractionally and he nodded, 'Sometimes,' with a reminiscent grin. 'At shows and the like, if there was a pigtailed little blonde directing her mount over the jumps with all the confidence in the world, then the memories would return and I'd find myself unconsciously watching the rest of the rounds to see how she fared.' His fingers ran through the silky strands clustering about her neck. 'It won't be long before your hair's that length again,' he smiled pleasurably.

A slightly perplexed look from the corner of her eye and Ashley queried, 'But I thought you said you preferred it short?'

'Of course I did,' he laughed with a teasing note that set her nerves tingling dramatically. 'How else was I going to make certain you'd let it grow?'

'Why, you cheat! I almost wish I'd kept it cut now,' she grinned mischievously.

Emerald green eyes held cornflower blue ones with a mock threat. 'But you won't!'

'I won't,' she was happy to agree before her expression turned thoughtful and she asked rather awkwardly, 'And —and Lucia—does she have long hair too?'

He drew a finger gently across her neck just below her ear. 'Somewhere around there, I think.'

'You think! Don't you know?' She had always believed Dane to be more observant than that—at least with someone who interested him.

'Not really,' he now informed her innocently, one corner of his shapely mouth starting to curve. 'You see, I don't usually pay that much attention to other men's wives.'

Other men's wives! Ashley was sure her mouth must have been gaping and she hurried to accuse, 'But Hal said she was your current girl-friend. And—and you didn't dispute it when I made much the same remark to you!'

Dane lifted his shoulders artlessly, without the least sign of discomposure. 'At the time it suited my purposes not to. I didn't think the idea of a little competition would do you any harm because I already knew from those occasions when I'd kissed you that you weren't, shall we say, alto-gether indifferent?—and so I decided to allow your mis-taken belief to stand,' he grinned unashamedly.

It was Ashley's turn to look threatening now as she re-called all those times she had almost been in tears at the thought of him making love to the other girl. But there was still one question left unanswered and she eyed him in puzzlement.

'Why would Hal think she was your girl-friend, then, if she was already married?' she frowned.

'Because the last time Hal came visiting, Lucia and I were going out together. Since then, however, we'd parted and in actual fact I attended her wedding to a neighbour of mine when I went back to collect the plane,' he disclosed casually.

'I wish I'd known that,' she murmured dolefully. 'I might have found some pleasure then in selecting all that furniture for you in Brisbane.'

'For *you*,' he corrected swiftly, but which was altered to, '*Us!*' just as rapidly by Ashley before she went on to reproach, 'I still think it was mean of you not to have given me any indication that I was buying it partly on my own behalf.'

'Hell! How many clues did you need?' he grinned, and ran a hand round the back of his neck in wonderment. 'From the very first night I came across to see you about the sale it must have been obvious I've hardly been able to keep my distance. You have a beautifully enticing mouth, my love,' as he bent his head to masterfully prove the point. Then he continued, 'And as if that wasn't enough, I then give you carte blanche to refurnish and decorate my home, as well as insisting that your awards for riding take pride of place in my office!'

'I thought you were only doing all those things in order to rile me!' she wailed defensively.

For a moment Dane's eyes closed, but when he opened them again they held a steady and implicit gleam. 'You reckon I couldn't have found a more direct method if that had been my objective?' he drawled.

'I guess so,' she gave a somewhat rueful laugh. 'Is that what you had in mind the night Mum went out with Ramsay and you said you'd shortly put a stop to my antagonising in one of two ways?'

'That's what I had in mind,' he confirmed expressively.

Secure in the knowledge that he loved her, Ashley felt safe this afternoon in enquiring interestedly, 'And just what were those alternatives?'

'That, in sheer frustration, I would either end up by beating the living daylights out of you as I did once before, or else I would be taking you to bed and making love to you until you didn't have the strength to fight me any more,' she was informed dryly.

'Oh!' Ashley's eyes widened and then began to sparkle outrageously. 'You also said I wouldn't like either suggestion. How wrong can you be?' she chuckled.

Dane's expression was just as tormenting as her own had been when he lowered his head to tease, 'That would depend entirely on which of the propositions you're talking about, wouldn't it?'

Once she might have been forced into retreat by such a remark—but not any more. Swinging her legs on to the seat, she knelt beside him, her fingers linking together at the back of his neck.

'I'll give you one guess,' she breathed huskily as her lips smoothed slowly over his in a seductive caress, but which swiftly developed into a deepening passion when Dane retaliated by pinning her against the back of the seat and devastated her emotions with the absorbing possessiveness of his response.

'I'm afraid, my love, that you make your clues too damned appealing for my self-discipline!' he groaned unsteadily quite some time later as he resolutely put her from him. 'So unless you want to be married in a very bright scarlet instead of white, I suggest you keep well over to your side and let me get us home,' bending forward to switch on the ignition once more.

Still kneeling, Ashley leant her upper arm along the back of the seat and rested her flushed cheek on the palm of her hand. 'Red suits me better than white does,' she couldn't resist teasing.

'Possibly,' Dane laughed, and stretched out an arm to briefly trail his fingertips along her jawline. 'But I think I'd like to see you in one of those frothy white creations which immediately send women hunting for their handkerchiefs, all the same.'

Ten weeks later Dane had his wish come true, and the morning after their wedding Ashley came back to consciousness slowly, drowsily, with the sound of the sea breaking rhythmically over the reef which surrounded their South Seas honeymoon island faintly penetrating into their bedroom. Stretching like a contented feline, she opened her eyes and smiled shyly on finding Dane already wide awake, his green gaze resting on her tenderly.

'I—I hope I was worth waiting for, after all,' she whispered throatily, not quite able to meet his eyes.

Dane rolled closer and dropped a feather-light kiss on the tip of her nose. 'Let's just say, I think I love you more today than I did yesterday . . . and I wouldn't have believed that was possible,' he divulged deeply.

Ashley's fingers slid wonderingly from his chest to wide shoulders, still finding it hard to believe that she was actually his wife, even though he had lovingly taught her just what that word could really mean last night.

'I wouldn't have believed I could love you as much as I do either!' she shook her head incredulously. 'You have no idea how I hated the idea of you buying Kindyerra.'

'Oh, yes, I have,' he contradicted wryly. 'You could hardly wait to order me off the place that first morning, if you remember.'

Her lips curved enchantingly. 'You shouldn't have said I was still a pert little brat,' she grinned. 'Anyway, you made sure you had the last word by putting that clause into the contract of sale.'

'I had to find some way of keeping you around, although I wasn't even certain myself why at the time. It just seemed like a good idea.' He bent his head and placed a lingering kiss at the base of her throat. 'Are you sorry?'

'Brokenhearted,' she gave the lie to her words with the bewitching smile which accompanied them. 'Or I very soon shall be if you don't convince me I'm not dreaming all of this.'

Dane was only too willing to oblige, and to Ashley's delight she found it wasn't a dream at all!

Harlequin

COLLECTION
EDITIONS OF 1978

Harlequin's Collection 1?

ANDREA BLAKE
**Night of
the Hurrica**

Harlequin's Collection 106   1.25

ANNE WEALE
**If This
Is Love**

**50 great stories
of special beauty
and significance**

$1.25
each novel

In 1976 we introduced the first 100 Harlequin
Collections—a selection of titles chosen from our
best sellers of the past 20 years. This series, a trip
down memory lane, proved how great romantic
fiction can be timeless and appealing from
generation to generation. The theme of love
and romance is eternal, and, when placed
in the hands of talented, creative, authors
whose true gift lies in their ability to write from the
heart, the stories reach a special level of brilliance
that the passage of time cannot dim. Like a
treasured heirloom, an antique of superb
craftsmanship, a beautiful gift from someone
loved—these stories too, have a special significance
that transcends the ordinary. **$1.25 each novel**

Here are your 1978
Harlequin Collection Editions...

Original Harlequin Romance numbers in brackets

ORDER FORM
Harlequin Reader Service

In U.S.A.
MPO Box 707
Niagara Falls, N.Y. 14302

In Canada
649 Ontario St.,
Stratford, Ontario, N5A 6W2

Please send me the following Harlequin Collection novels. I am enclosing my check or money order for $1.25 for each novel ordered, plus 25¢ to cover postage and handling.

☐ 102	☐ 115	☐ 128	☐ 140
☐ 103	☐ 116	☐ 129	☐ 141
☐ 104	☐ 117	☐ 130	☐ 142
☐ 105	☐ 118	☐ 131	☐ 143
☐ 106	☐ 119	☐ 132	☐ 144
☐ 107	☐ 120	☐ 133	☐ 145
☐ 108	☐ 121	☐ 134	☐ 146
☐ 109	☐ 122	☐ 135	☐ 147
☐ 110	☐ 123	☐ 136	☐ 148
☐ 111	☐ 124	☐ 137	☐ 149
☐ 112	☐ 125	☐ 138	☐ 150
☐ 113	☐ 126	☐ 139	☐ 151
☐ 114	☐ 127		

Number of novels checked @
$1.25 each = $ _____

N.Y. and N.J. residents add
appropriate sales tax $ _____

Postage and handling $ _____.25

TOTAL $ _____

NAME _____
                    (Please Print)
ADDRESS _____

CITY _____

STATE/PROV. _____

ZIP/POSTAL CODE _____

AB ROM 2248

Offer expires June 30, 1979